The Baker's Daughter
Braving Evil in WW II Berlin

by

D. P. Cornelius

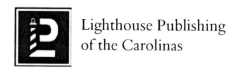

Lighthouse Publishing
of the Carolinas

THE BAKER'S DAUGHTER, BRAVING EVIL IN WW II BERLIN BY D.P. CORNELIUS
Published by Lighthouse Publishing of the Carolinas
2333 Barton Oaks Dr., Raleigh, NC, 27614

ISBN: 978-1-946016-10-2
Copyright © 2017 by D. P. Cornelius
Cover design by Elaina Lee, www.forthemusedesign.com
Interior design by Atritex, www.atritex.com

Available in print from your local bookstore, online, or from the publisher at: https://lpcbooks.com

For more information on this book and the author visit: dpcornelius.com

Brought to you by the creative team at Lighthouse Publishing of the Carolinas: Christine Richards, Rowena Kuo, Eddie Jones, Shonda Savage, Meaghan Burnett, Lucie Winborne, Ann Tatlock, and Brian Cross.

Library of Congress Cataloging-in-Publication Data
Cornelius, D.P.
The Baker's Daughter, Braving Evil in WW II Berlin / D.P. Cornelius 1st ed.

Printed in the United States of America

PRAISE FOR *THE BAKER'S DAUGHTER, BRAVING EVIL IN WW II BERLIN*

D.P. Cornelius tells a story based on recent history, but it's also based on a bigger story that goes back even further. The young characters take risks to show that in the darkest times, love is what saves us.

~ **Dean Nelson, Ph.D.**
Founder and Director, Writer's Symposium by the Sea
Point Loma Nazarene University
San Diego, CA

The Baker's Daughter, D.P. Cornelius's debut Christian novel, quickly pulls the reader into a story filled with intrigue, danger, family loyalty, and sacrifice. Cornelius's characters are complex and multi-faceted, his storyline filled with unexpected twists as life in WWII Berlin unfolds. Within the war-ravaged city, under the eerie wail of air raid sirens, the baker's family struggles to keep their bakery open. Daughter Liddy comes of age as she befriends the young Polish immigrant who steps in to help at her family's bakery. When his secrets are revealed, Liddy and her family face increasing threats from the Nazi regime, and Liddy must figure out how to protect and then save the young man who has captured her heart. Her courage brings her to a showdown with the Nazi officer who has his own secrets. An unforgettable story of bravery, sacrifice, and love.

~ **Stacy Monson**
Author of the multi-award winning series, Chain of Lakes
2016 National Excellence in Romance
2016 Bookbuyers Best Inspirational

D.P. Cornelius wraps history, intrigue, suspense, and the gospel into a novel that is compelling and motivating for any age. He challenges us in practical ways to know what we believe and to stand up for it. *The Baker's Daughter* will teach and challenge his target audience of young teens throughout the book as well as with well-designed follow-up questions. This story is perfect for homeschoolers and faith-based schools—and their parents. I highly recommend it.

~ Tim Olson
Life Coach, Teacher, Pastor, and Author

An amazing fictional story. This book will keep the reader up at night as one exciting and surprising scene shifts to another. In addition, there are spiritual struggles that result in transformation, thrilling the soul. Enjoy your read. You will like to come back for more.

~ Dr. David W. McQuoid
Author of *JUST DAVE, JUST PAPA: Encountering the God of Grace Through the Joys and Challenges of Life*

Acknowledgments

I am most grateful to Eddie Jones, Cindy Sproles, and the entire team at Lighthouse Publishing of the Carolinas for the opportunity provided to me. My goodness, they have grown their ministry as a resource to the prospective new writer!

My interest in writing historical fiction came to me late in life. Retirement provided the time; God provided the inspiration. What started as a curiosity about two Christian martyrs, Bonhoeffer and Kolbe, turned into a delightful trip wherein I discovered many others who felt compelled to confront evil during WW II. Grounded with all these difference-makers, the story then evolved.

A wonderful writers' group at my church, Church of the Open Door (Maple Grove, MN), led by Stacy Monson, Nina Engen, and Eric Therkilsen, has nurtured and encouraged me the past few years. The group has grown tremendously, with some who have come and gone, but I am thankful to each one who has made helpful comments along the way.

A number of writing and editing professionals provided excellent input—ranging from suggestions to edited improvements. My heartfelt thanks go to Kerri Kennedy, Karen Autio, Rowena Kuo, Terri Kelly, Andrea Merrell, Marsha Hubler, and Chris Richards—all of whom contributed to making *The Baker's Daughter, Braving Evil in WW II Berlin* a better book. And finally, beta readers Nikole and Emma McCauley, and Leslie and Amanda Cornelius, put their eagle eyes to great use with their final review.

My family—wife Leslie, son Brian, and daughter Cristina, provided early story feedback and encouragement along the way. They constantly reminded me that God's timeline was different from mine. Of course, when various roadblocks presented themselves, I turned to my Father God. He always provided the answers. Without a doubt, at the end of the story, Scripture promised that love would prevail!

Dedication

I dedicate this book to my family: wife Leslie, son Brian, and daughter Cristina, who have all been instrumental in my faith journey—a precursor to writing this story.

Love always protects, always trusts, always hopes, always perseveres. Love never fails.
(1 Corinthians 13:7–8)

Chapter 1

June 1943
Near Warsaw, Poland

Marek heard the vehicles pull up, shattering the silence. The squeal of their brakes—one, then another, then once more. Three of them. Stomping boots hit the ground, doors slammed.

In the still of the deserted building, he stretched out flat on a storage platform above the warehouse, his heart racing, his muscles tightening. The raid had come early. Now, for him, it was too late. No turning back. They'd be right below him in a flash. *Please, God, don't let them see me.*

"Break that door down," came the order from outside. A window pane shattered, rifle butts banged on metal, and the door popped free. File drawers slid open, one after another. Reams of paper plopped to the floor.

Marek peered over the edge of the platform. There stood the printing press he'd operated for almost a year. Like a good friend, he'd come to know her quirks. Now he was back to save her. Could a person have a bond with a piece of machinery? *Must be so.* Why else would he be here? Yes, he knew how to sneak in and hide. But who would take such a risk? Marek Menkowitz would. He cherished his press. He called her *Schatzi.*

Several minutes later, he heard the call from a man in the office—okay to proceed to the factory. Marek dared not look down but lay still. *What will be next in their path of destruction?* He winced as the sounds of ransacking filled the air—the incessant dinging, clanging, and pinging of sledgehammers, the echoing drone of continued blows of metal on metal. Had *Schatzi* been spared? Had his plan worked? Marek was rather proud of his plan. He had prepared the machine in advance, disguising her like she was already ransacked. He had cut the drive belt, turned over the keyboard, lay disconnected parts askew, and pounded dents into panels. She was in total disarray—a most marvelous act of disguise for a machine that could easily be put back to work.

****

All that was just a distant memory now. Marek couldn't count how many times that memory had flashed into his mind. Disguise was a part of the times. *Things are not always the way they seem.* That's what his father had told him many a time. And now as a teenager, it was well implanted in his head.

Sitting perched on a stool in the kitchen of Biermann's Restaurant, he was reminded of that now as he stared at some pastries he had made. They looked scrumptious. The sugar dusting on the top beckoned the hungry, especially those with a sweet tooth. But Marek knew in the tasting, there'd be huge disappointment.

More than a few times, he had overheard customers yelling in the front room, "These are so tasteless!" Always loud enough so someone in the kitchen might hear. That's what happens when you cut the sugar in half. That's what happens when sugar is in such short supply. He could not fathom why the customers kept coming back.

Some years ago, Father Kolbe had taught him how to make pastries the right way. Fortunately, he had also taught him to operate a printing press. Now deceased at the hands of the Nazis, Franciscan Father Maximilian Kolbe was no doubt eternally grateful for Marek's earlier act of disguise. On that day in late November over three years ago, when Nazi soldiers ransacked the father's city, what some called the "City of Mary," they were fooled. The Nazis walked right by *Schatzi*, no doubt in search of other things more ripe for the ravaging.

It was one of many presses at the grand monastery, the largest in the world, where the newspaper, *The Knight*, was printed, then distributed to thousands in many countries.

A clang of a pan in a nearby sink interrupted Marek's train of thought. He looked over to see Heinrich, a seventy-year-old compatriot in the kitchen.

"Hey, Heinrich," Marek yelled out. "Remember when we worked together over at Father Kolbe's monastery?"

"Yes, why do you ask?" The gray-haired man stopped scrubbing the pan and turned around. "I was there eight years going back to 1931." Even from a distance, Marek could see the deep creases on his forehead, confirmation of what he always thought. Heinrich was someone who had thoroughly experienced life.

"Ah, help me remember some of the details. Your wise old brain can probably retrieve them better than my distracted young one. So when did Father Kolbe get sent into exile?"

"That was just after the Germans invaded in September 1939. The authorities quietly shut the place down at the time. Father Kolbe discharged most of us, reminding us to 'forget not love.' He then was sent to a nearby work camp."

"That's when we both ended up over here at the restaurant, right? It wasn't more than a few months after that I got a tip from a customer that the monastery would be ransacked the next day."

"Yes. They released the father after a few months, so he came back, only to find it in shambles. He was able to rebuild some things, but they were not allowed to publish anymore. The focus then became turning it into a refuge—a home for over three thousand people. Little did the Nazis realize almost half of them were Jews."

"We did it *all* there, didn't we?" Marek said. "Not just baking and printing. We grew vegetables. I remember we repaired everything from shoes to farm tools. There was a pharmacy, as well as a small hospital. The father even started plans for a radio station. It really became a city unto itself," Marek added. "But Father Kolbe kept petitioning to print again, didn't he?"

"Yes, he was finally allowed to print one more edition at the end of 1940. Father Kolbe was delighted."

Warmth rushed through Marek. His prayers had been answered. He knew that *Schatzi* must have been the trusty machine that had come back to life to print for the father once again—this time the last edition of *The Knight*.

Heinrich continued: "Then came Father Kolbe's second arrest early in 1941. That was the final blow, foreshadowing the end of the 'City of Mary.' This time, the father was sent to Auschwitz."

"I recall that his final edition of *The Knight* had some comments about truth."

"Yes," the old man added. "Father Kolbe declared one of his core beliefs: 'the truth is the truth.'" Heinrich smiled. "There's more to that than you think. The father said that 'no one in the world can change truth. What we can do and should do is to seek truth and serve it when we have found it.' Although he did not say it directly, I think it was obvious. No one could deny the truth of the day."

"And what is that?" Marek asked.

"That Nazism is evil."

"That's right. You are indeed wise, Heinrich. I've learned that no matter what a person's pastry skills, sugarcoating will not work." With a wink, he tilted his head back. He knew there was no way he could sugarcoat his job atop a stool in the restaurant kitchen. It could not compare with the one he craved next to a press like *Schatzi*.

****

Liddy recognized the handwriting on the envelope. Had her grandmother intentionally left the opened letter on top of the pile on the counter? Before she could pick it up, the noise of rustling from the nearby bedroom prompted Liddy to move back to the chair at the kitchen table. She sat down and pulled a picture album closer.

"*Guten morgen*, Liddy. You're already at that album? My goodness, you've put a lot of time into those pictures since you've been here."

"It's only been two weeks, *Grossmutter*." She leaned in toward the table.

"Well, it seems you're always fussing over them."

"That's when I'm not taking the actual pictures," Liddy responded with a smile.

"Let's have a look. What are your favorites today?" Her grandmother pulled out a chair and sat down beside her. The frayed edge of the sleeve of her bathrobe caught Liddy's eye. That was unlike her. Probably something she had come to live with since the war began.

"I should think about starting breakfast," her grandmother said. "But it will just have to wait. Your poor *Grossvater* had nothing but toast. He was so intent on getting out of here early. He wanted to get there when the doors opened."

"Get where?" She crossed her arms.

"The office where they manage records for estates. I'm not sure what they call it. Things have really been a mess—straightening out your Uncle Friedrich's will. God rest his soul."

"This is indeed a cruel war. Why did it have to take someone as nice as Uncle Friedrich? The Lord only knows. Uncle was always so generous to me. Not many people can afford to go to college these days, especially a fine teaching school like Ludwig here in Munich. I can't wait till the fall." Liddy pushed the stack of pictures that depicted buildings only, off to the side.

Her grandmother pulled another pile toward her. "These are the ones I like," she said. "Countryside and scenery. I don't understand why you take all those shots of buildings." She held up a photo of a building. "This looks familiar, but I can't place it."

"They represent history, *Grossmutter.* Don't you see? They're part of the very fabric of our country's heritage. Someday, I want to compile a picture book of historical buildings throughout Germany."

"Well, I would still rather look at these. They're prettier." She became distracted by a thread on the sleeve of her bathrobe, pulling on it, then stopping.

"To each her own," Liddy replied. "There's just so much history in the structures." She paused, then resumed. "So, *Grossmutter*. I've been meaning to ask you something. I hope you don't mind my snooping, but I noticed a letter on the counter."

"Yes?" A resigned look commandeered her face.

"I know my father's handwriting when I see it." She tapped her knuckles on the table.

"Oh, you're right, dear. I was going to talk to you about it. Your father has enlisted my help."

"No doubt because he's tired of asking me directly." Liddy took a pained breath and closed her eyes.

"Probably." She paused, then continued, "Listen, Liddy. You must understand. Things have really gotten dire there at the bakery. They just lost a young girl they'd hired. Was only there three weeks."

"I know. Each time I talk with Father, he brings it up. And each time I tell him the same thing—I want to be a schoolteacher, a history teacher."

"But couldn't you just put that off for a while?" Her shining eyes looked wide.

"*Grossmutter*, what time is it? Eight thirty? No matter how many times I've done it in the past at the bakery, I can't drag myself out of bed each day at four o'clock in the morning. I haven't even eaten breakfast this morning."

"Speaking of that, I'd better get it started. I have a special treat for you. I know how much you love it."

"Tell me." Liddy's eyebrows raised.

"Could I interest you in some bacon, young lady?"

"No!" Liddy squealed. "How did you get that?"

"I had to pay dearly, but you're worth it."

"Fantastic. And *Grossvater's* going to miss out on all this?"

"We'll save him a piece of bacon, though I know that will be hard to do." Her voice was bubbly.

Her grandmother arose from her chair. The clang from pulling out the frying pan meant it would not be long before that bacon would be making good company with some bright-eyed eggs. Once the cooking was well underway, Liddy peered over her grandmother's shoulder, staring at the pan.

"I would help you, *Oma*, but you know what a poor cook I am. Besides, those eggs look more awake than me."

"Well, if you had that kind of heat beneath your underside, you'd be awake too." They both chuckled. The oil in the pan seemed to sputter in agreement.

"I tell you what you can do," her *Oma* continued. "Clean off that table. You can move all those pictures over to the counter here. And put some silverware out."

"All right." Liddy paused for a moment. "Too bad we don't have some of Father's famous pastries. I can taste them now." Liddy's tongue made a quick pass across her lips, now moist.

"See, there you go. If you were back at the bakery, you could have them every day."

"I know, *Grossmutter*. I love the aromas there, but that's about the only thing. You know what? I can't stand to knead dough. That squishy stuff oozing between my fingers. Flour dustings all over my face. Not to mention all the clean-up afterward. The sticky residue of the dough on my hands is good for only one thing—hanging on to the broom handle. No wonder Willy never wants to sweep after me. Then there is dealing with the public. People can be so demanding, especially in the morning. Chances are they didn't get any real coffee that day."

"Oh, come now. It can't be all *that* bad." *Oma* deftly deposited the eggs and bacon onto two plates and carried them to the table. She sat down by Liddy and looked her straight in the eye. "Your family needs you, Liddy. Don't you miss them? What about young Willy? He needs a big sister to guide him."

"Yes, but then I do have you and *Grossvater* here in Munich." Liddy reached over to squeeze her *Oma's* hand. Just as she did that, her *grossmutter's* cat jumped up onto her lap as if jealous.

"Besides, your sweet little kitty here has grown so fond of me." She petted the cat with tender strokes. *Oma* stared at them both with admiring eyes.

"We love you very much, Liddy. We'd cherish the idea of having you stay with us here, but your father needs you more in Berlin. Please …"

Chapter 2

M arek looked forward to coming home from his work at the restaurant. Mother would be busy preparing a meal. Father would be resting on the couch, a fresh cup of hot tea by his side. He started work early at 6:00 at the toolmaking factory, so he relished the opportunity to relax before dinner.

On this Monday, however, the long trip home was more eventful and much more disturbing. A new level of uneasiness had taken over the streets in Warsaw. The looks in people's eyes haunted him. They brought back memories of the previous October when there was rampant fear, screaming, and helplessness. That's when mostly Jewish folks, including women and children, were rounded up in the streets. Gunshots—people killed right there on the spot. All in all, horrific, unspeakable acts by some humans—or at least that's what they called themselves—toward their fellow man.

Marek trembled as he entered his apartment building. He hurried to unlock the family's mailbox, as was his practice this time of day. He fumbled through the four letters, and one caught his eye. There it was—the letter from Wilensky Printing Company. Ripping the envelope open, he read the news he had so long awaited. They were offering him a job. He could start next week. He wanted to shout, "Hallelujah," but it just wouldn't come out. Worries about what might happen next in the street took over. Nevertheless, he could not wait to tell his parents. His stride consumed three steps at a time as he rushed up to the fourth floor. He inserted the key but found the door already unlocked. He burst inside.

"Father, Mother!" No response. He shouted again. Silence. He darted from room to room, calling their names. His voice strident, his breathing ragged. Had they gone somewhere? They would tell him. Half a stalk of celery unchopped on the cutting board. Half a cup of tea sat on the table. *They're gone.* He poked his finger into the dark liquid. *Still warm.*

****

Liddy pulled the sheet and blanket off of the couch and began to fold them up—part of her daily routine while at her grandparents' in Munich. The door to the bathroom opened, and *Oma* came out, the belt of her bathrobe pulled tight, the fragrance of some fresh soap trailing in the air as she sauntered to the bedroom and closed the door behind her.

Liddy headed down the hall toward the bathroom, also eager to get cleaned up for the day. The smell of bacon lingered, then became more intense. A flash of light brightened the hallway. Liddy turned to see flames leaping from the pan of bacon grease.

"*Oma*, help!" She shouted as loud as she could. *What horror—the flames are spreading to some napkins.*

"Help!" Liddy yelled again as she rushed to find a saucepan. She held it under the faucet. Her *Grossmutter*, half-dressed, rushed out of her bedroom.

"Oh my, Liddy—what's happened?" A shaky hand rushed to her forehead as she ran toward the bathroom. "Did I forget to shut the burner off?" She soon returned with a large towel. "Here, this is still damp."

Liddy poured water on the flames, but many leapt out of the pan. A cloud of steam hissed and hovered. She grabbed the towel from *Oma's* hands and hurled it out over the flames, then refilled the pan. In desperation, she flung the new load of water over the stove, drenching the nearby counter as well.

At last, the fire had been extinguished. Liddy exhaled loudly. She looked over at her *Grossmutter*, whose breathing was heavy. "Are you all right, *Oma?*"

"Yes," came her shaking voice in between breaths. "I feel so foolish. How could I have left that burner on?"

"Don't worry, *Oma*. Everything's going to be all right," Liddy said as she surveyed the damage. She looked at the treasure reserved for *Grossvater*—the piece of bacon, on a paper napkin next to the burner, was now black and shriveled. "I hope he likes it crisp," she said as she held it up. Her emotions were jumbled. *Would she cry or would she laugh?* Her emerging smile raised the corners of her *Oma's* mouth as well. They hugged. *Maybe a bit of humor would assuage some of their despair.*

Then Liddy's heart sank. "Oh no! This can't be." She spotted her stacks of photos and rushed to pick them up. Her shaking hands held up clumps of wet, greasy pictures stuck together, as she shook her head in disbelief.

"Oh, no, no, *no*," her defiant cry came bursting out. "Why, Lord, why?" She paced back and forth, then threw the soggy pictures down. "I just can't deal with this anymore. It will all have to wait."

She dabbed at her teary eyes and headed to the bathroom.

Grossvater walked in later that morning, surprised to find the remnants of the kitchen fire. "Left the burner on, huh?" *Oma* and Liddy sat quietly, consoling each other on the couch. Now that the commotion was over, the cat had come out of hiding to join them.

Oma was the first to speak. "Yes. One horrible mess, wouldn't you say, Gunter? How could I have done this?"

"Are you both okay?"

"Yeah, we saved you a piece of bacon. Over there on the counter." Liddy pointed.

Grossvater looked back toward the mess, then shook his head as if to say, "No, thanks."

"Well, at least it's only property—that can be fixed," he said. "Praise God that no one was hurt. Or think about what might have happened if the whole apartment building had caught on fire." He surveyed the damage. "I don't know how best to get all this grease and soot off."

"We had a fire like this at the bakery once," Liddy added. "That was way back before Willy was even born. I should call Father for advice."

"That's a good idea," *Grossvater* replied. "But before you do that, maybe we should talk about something else that turned out bad today. I hate to even bring it up." He moved to sit down across from them.

"No, Gunter, something else on top of all this? What could be worse?" Her shoulders curled forward.

"Oh, I don't know that I can discuss it with Liddy here." He looked over at his granddaughter, his eyes welling up.

"It's about your Uncle Friedrich's money." His voice sounded shaky as he leaned forward in his chair. "The accounts don't show any funds left for college. Zero."

"What?" Liddy screeched. She jumped to her feet and stared at her *Grossvater*.

"Can't be. Must be some mistake," *Oma* implored, her jaw jutting out. "Friedrich told us last December there's a tidy sum there. I can't believe he would lie. Our son?" She fidgeted with a button on her blouse.

"No, *Grossvater*, Uncle Friedrich wouldn't lie. What's happened to it?" She chewed at her lower lip.

"I just don't know, sweetheart. All I can say is the account now shows zero. I tried to get a history of statements, but to no avail."

The tears streamed down Liddy's face. She grabbed a pillow off the couch and buried her head in it.

Not until later that afternoon did Liddy feel ready to call her father.

"It's the worst day of my life, Father!" The muscles in her hand strained as she clutched the phone. "Yes, yes, I know you want me home … What? … Well, first there was this fire in the kitchen … No, everyone is fine … *Oma* left the bacon grease over the lit burner … Yes, that's right. And all my photos—ruined! It was a mess for sure. But the worst thing, Father—Uncle Friedrich's money for me. It's gone! …Yes, the college fund—there's no money. Zero … I don't know what's happened. No, we just don't know yet … But, Father, I'm no use to you at the bakery. My heart's just not into it. I wanted to become a teacher." Liddy began sobbing. After a moment, she cleared her voice, and it came out more measured and soft. "Remember, Father. Remember? You always said I needed to break out of my shell, right? … I so wanted to be on my own … Yes, I heard you lost your help. Say what? What? You're going to the prison at Tegel? Father!"

****

The rhythmic rumble of the train's wheels had been mesmerizing, enough so that Marek's head, propped against the window, had begun to bob. But a turn of the train to the south brought the rays from the setting sun straight into his eyes, and he awoke from his stupor. Outside the window, a shroud of haze formed around trees soon left far behind. A different sort of haze seemed to linger in his mind.

Marek adjusted his tired body. He found little comfort on the hard wooden seats in the third-class cabin. His was a body that craved deep sleep. But it was in a fight with a mind that kept bringing up visions of the events of the last three days. And besides, keeping his eyes closed just might discourage a conductor who might ask questions he wasn't prepared to answer. Well, at least he wasn't a freeloader—he had a ticket all the way to Berlin.

What to do at the border crossing was another thing. Could he hide underneath the car between the wheels as the train pulled into the station—only to sneak away in the dark so nobody would see him? Easy to imagine, but hard to pull off. At least, that's what his good sense told him.

Besides, Marek had already summoned up more courage than he thought a seventeen-year-old was supposed to have when he made the gut-wrenching decision to leave home. He still struggled to comprehend that his family was really gone. But who knew when any of them would return. Now, he had no choice—he really didn't. He had to head toward some sort of stability. Chaos had taken over Warsaw.

Marek's mind flashed forward to the present. He reached into his pocket and pulled out his identification papers. If only looking at them one more time would make them perfect. He took a deep breath and looked up. *Please, God,* he implored, *make the agent at the border crossing an old lady with failing eyesight.* During wartime they wouldn't waste able-bodied men for such jobs, would they? Maybe at night she would just go through the motions and pass him right through. Or perhaps he could distract her with charming talk. He was rather proud of how well he spoke German for a Polish lad.

Images of the last few days' events continued to push themselves to the front of Marek's mind. Who left home without saying good-bye to his parents? What about his best friend, Micah? He was a strong, determined young fellow. He would be okay, wouldn't he?

Outside the window, strong gusts of wind whipped the leaves, clinging fast to the swaying branches of the trees. But they were prepared for that. Those trees could depend on well-grounded roots that would hold fast through the worst of storms. In a few months, those leaves would fall, but there would be a renewal of life in the spring. A predictable life with four seasons. At that moment, a strain of jealousy coursed through Marek's veins for, of all things, the predictability of nature. He had no such assurance of the future. Completely uprooted, he was filled with doubt. When and where would he find new roots?

The steady chugging of the locomotive eventually brought him a sense of calm. At least he was headed away from the chaos in Warsaw. Since the Germans had invaded and taken over a few years earlier, his world had been turned upside down. But determined to get through the war, he would be a survivor.

Marek dared to take a good look at his surroundings. The luggage rack teemed with bags of various sizes and colors, the air thick and heavy with cigarette smoke. The distinct odor of weary travelers filled every nook and cranny in the overcrowded car.

Across the aisle from him was a family of four with two small children, their faces flushed with anxiety, not youthful joy. *What is their story?* He doubted they were off to see their grandparents. No, they were in escape mode too. His glance roamed the car, looking at the different faces—faces whose eyes shifted away. Everyone had a story. Maybe some were similar to his, but no one seemed anxious to share their story. Nor, for that matter, did he want to ask them.

Marek pulled a stained business card with frayed edges out of his pocket. God willing, he would find some stability—in Berlin, of all places, the very center of the mighty Third Reich. Hunker down—that's what he had come to believe he needed to do for a season. Now he was only a few short hours away from the place where he would try to do just that. But could he even remember how to find the address? It had been so many years since he had been there. He glanced at the card:

Saul Rosenberg

"Supplier of Paper and Ink Products to the Newsprint Industry"

1432 Reinig Strasse N.

Berlin, Germany

****

The light glared off the stout lady's heavy thick glasses, their rims splayed outward by her wide face. A broad nose kept them from sliding down. Marek prayed the dim light at her table would keep her from focusing on his papers. Her uniform was quite wrinkled. Did that reveal someone less observant of details?

"Born in Warsaw," she said with a quick glance upward. "Have you not traveled before, young man? These papers look too fresh, hardly used. But the issue date on them is almost two years ago."

Marek's head jerked up. "Oh, well, er … yes. I am very careful about how I keep my papers, my dear *Frau*." Why had he picked that date? "In fact," he hurried to add, "my father once called me fastidious." A nervous chuckle followed.

Her eyes peered over the top of her glasses. "What is your business in Germany?"

"I have relatives in Berlin." Marek sniffled as he looked down. "I just lost my aunt. I'm headed to the funeral." Marek knew full well that his aunt had died over a year ago. No matter now. Couldn't this woman before him be someone's aunt herself? Would she cooperate in sympathy?

An expectant moment of silence was broken by the loud sound of a stamp striking his papers with authority. *What a sweet sound*, Marek thought as he stepped ahead.

****

The weather was unusually cool for late June. The din of the train station in Munich added to the numbness that had taken ahold of Liddy. She marched on through the crowd, not aware that her *Grossvater* struggled as he lugged her suitcases three paces behind. Her head was in a fog, except for one thing.

"What is your destination, *Fraulein*?" the woman at the ticket window asked.

"One ticket to Berlin, please."

Chapter 3

Liddy carried a tray of fresh-baked *streuselkuchen, schnecken,* and *berliners* from the kitchen and set them down with a thump on top of the display case. The noise was loud enough to divert her mother's attention from the customer she was helping. Liddy forced a smile in their direction. In the back of her mind, she could hear her father's voice proclaiming the importance of the customer. But it was her father's actual voice and face she longed for. He was due home any minute, and she was anxious to hear how his new night job had gone. Willy was still too young to think about such things and had gone back to his bedroom. As she looked out the window, she caught her father's familiar profile, but his stride revealed weariness. He squinted in the early morning sun, no doubt looking with pride at the namesake sign that read, "Mittendorf Bakery." Liddy tucked some loose strands back in her ponytail and took a quick glance at her apron. She hoped she didn't appear too frazzled. Even though she was not happy to be back at the bakery, creating extra worry for the father she adored was the last thing she wanted to do.

"Mm-m," Father said as he walked in. "That aroma of fresh-baked *streuselkuchen* must mean something is going right, Renate."

Mother gave him a quick glance that turned into a sigh of relief. *"Guten morgen*, Klaus," she said, then returned to help a customer. A customer—that was a good sign. Too few of them had prompted Father to start the new nightshift job at the prison in Tegel to bring in more money. Liddy thought back to the telephone call from Munich to her father. What a relief it had been to find out he was just working there!

"How did it go?" Liddy asked with a smile.

"It went okay," Father said, as he scratched a night's worth of stubble that shadowed the curve of his chin. "More important—how did you all fare here?"

As the customer passed by on her way out with her baked goods, she gave him a quick nod.

He responded, *"Guten morgen, Frau* Meyer. Thank you for stopping in. Come back soon."

Mother came from behind the counter. Assisted by a black cane, she shuffled along. While the muscles in her right hand strained to get a firm grasp of the cane, she wiped her left hand back and forth against the front of her white apron. That added a few more stains to those no doubt left over from the day before. Liddy lamented how her mother was definitely looking older than her forty-eight years—a thin woman with hair prematurely gray. Yet Liddy swelled with pride. She knew that even with a face full of wrinkles, her mother's every move reflected an energy that belied the pain deep inside.

"I guess we did all right too," Mother said, but her tone betrayed the truth. "Well, we didn't exactly make the best team. I'm sure Liddy would admit that she cannot follow recipes very well, and my arthritic hands make it difficult to knead the dough. Maybe we need to switch roles."

"I wish the dough would knead itself. I don't like doing it either," Liddy said, but her mother appeared not to pay attention.

"Taking care of the customer is what is really important," Mother said. "We can't forget the counterwork when they come in. The customer comes first."

Liddy thought about dealing with the customers—how that was not a role well suited to her either. She wished the words would come right to her so she could talk to them with ease.

"Bread and pastries that taste good—that's still what it comes down to," said Father. His lips formed a thin line of worry tinged with resignation. "No doubt we all have to do our best under these more difficult circumstances. What about Willy? Did he help today?"

"Oh, you can't expect too much from an eight-year-old," Mother said. "He rounded up ingredients and helped with the cleanup. Getting him up and out of bed was half the battle this morning."

Liddy searched for something to take the focus off her little brother. "So tell us, Father, what was it like as a prison guard? Were you ever afraid?"

"No. Not on the first day anyway. You have to remember that most of the inmates are sleeping, and they are pretty well behaved. What might they be up to, after all? To tell you the truth, I'm more afraid of an air raid than the prisoners."

"What would you do?" Mother asked. "Do they have a shelter?"

"They have a make-do shelter on the lower level for the guards and staff, but they tell me first we would have to move the prisoners from the third floor down to the second floor. I shudder to think of the first night when those sirens go off. We'll have to see how it all goes."

Liddy looked at her mother, whose face at that moment seemed to take on a new layer of worry.

"Well, I don't like the sound of it at all," Mother said, her voice filled with concern. "But I guess we have to do what we have to do—all thanks to our glorious *führer*, Adolph Hitler." She cast a sarcastic scowl.

Father stared at Mother and scowled back. "Be careful what you're saying in public," he said in a soft voice, as he checked that no one else had come in. "Remember, dear, we had this conversation before. We get the extra money we sorely need, and at some point, they may start to draft older men into the army. I need a vital job like the one at the prison. Then I should be safe from the dangers of the battlefield."

With a resigned look, Father scanned the room. He sighed and shook his head. He seemed tired and more than ready to collapse from the long night, but there was still plenty of work to do. Two of the three small tables were covered with dishes and wadded-up napkins, and the floor cried out for a good sweeping.

Liddy loaded the glass case with pastries while her mother coaxed the last few drops out of the coffee pot. "Not a drop wasted," was a phrase Liddy had heard often during these times of severe shortages.

With her cup shaking, Mother slumped into a wooden chair at the nearest table. Its legs screeched on the floor from the force of her weak body collapsing into the chair.

Liddy watched with anxiety as her mother's uneasiness meant she had found little comfort. At least Mother was off her feet after an exhausting full morning of work.

Liddy took a moment to reflect. She had wished she were at college in Munich. Since coming back, friends of her parents commented on how difficult it would be to keep the bakery running.

Maybe they were right. But now that she was committed to her parents, she had made up her mind to prove them wrong. Yes, as family-owned bakeries go, this was not a very large place. With the constraints of wartime, it barely had enough of a middle class from which to draw its clientele, mostly good folks from the northeast Berlin borough of Pankow. But the front customer area with tables for those who wanted to linger with a pastry and beverage could accommodate only about a half-dozen people. The kitchen, without a doubt, had become the center of Liddy and her family's lives. Thank heavens, they could escape to a few quiet spots.

The main level of the building hosted a side room with two comfortable chairs, a desk, a reading lamp, and a pull-out sofa that her mother used once in a while if she could not make the trek upstairs to the bedrooms at night. Liddy's parents enjoyed the room's bookshelf and upright piano. Liddy remembered the times when Mother had been able to play the piano rather well. But no longer— the pain in her arthritic hands had put a stop to that.

Liddy now worried about her father. Could he cope with having two jobs? He had gone to analyze the stack of dirty pots and pans in the kitchen and now came back into the main room. He grabbed the balustrade of the stairway and moved up a few steps as if to give his voice added authority. "Willy," he yelled, "we really could use some help down here cleaning up!"

In seconds, Willy came bounding down the stairs. Unlike the others in his family, he exploded with energy. Getting up early may have been a problem, but by 8:30, he was raring to go. "Hi, Father. Can I practice the piano this morning? I can help with the cleanup afterward. By the time you head for bed, all will be quiet."

"Well … I don't know," Father said. Piano practice was far down on his priority list. The piano had seen plenty of use in years past, mostly by Mother. Its dark-stained but faded upright body contrasted sharply with the row of white keys, even though they, too, were no longer at their brightest.

Yes, indeed, Liddy thought. *The piano had seen better times.* For years, it had found a happy home in the church basement, and many a Sunday they had eyed it. They were delighted when the pastor was able to upgrade, making it available to them.

When it came to piano playing, Willy was not to be denied. Next, he pursued his request with Mother. "Oh, please? Mother, can I?"

Liddy had a hunch how Mother would respond. An anxious query usually worked. Willy, with stubby fingers and small hands, was not the prototypical young piano player. Yet, the whole family was proud of him, and his desire seemed to make up for any physical shortcomings.

"Well, I suppose so, son," Mother replied. The smile on her face reminded Liddy of how much joy the piano brought to her mother's heart. She knew Mother yearned to hear its wonderful musical tones, ever since she was no longer able to create those melodies herself. However imperfect the strokes of Willy's stubby fingers, they all recognized that he, nevertheless, had some talent. And, unlike her mother's fingers, his were willing and able. His playing somehow brought a magical peace to the house, at least in her parents' minds, the kind of magic needed to drown out the harsh clamor of the world outside the door—that of war-torn Berlin.

Chapter 4

In the bakery, Renate gave the young man a quick once-over from head to toe. A puzzled expression masked her face as she tried to recollect having seen him before. *Was it here at the bakery? No, he must be a complete stranger,* she concluded. When he asked to see Klaus, she shot back, "Is he expecting you?"

"Well, not exactly," the lad replied. "I'm responding to his Help Wanted notice on the wall at the grocery store. It said to apply in person."

"Well, he just came home from his night job. Wait a moment, please," Renate said. She shook her head. Still puzzled, she did an about-face to hail her husband. "Klaus," she called to the kitchen, "there's somebody here to see you." She then headed to a nearby table and began to clear it, but made a point to stay within earshot.

Klaus emerged from the kitchen, rubbing his hands dry with a towel. "Hello," he said to the young man, "you must be here about the job. What's your name?"

"Marek Menkowicz. I saw your notice for someone with bakery experience. I learned while at a monastery near Warsaw."

"Fine," Klaus said. He then turned toward Renate. "Marek, this is my wife, Renate." She was happy to be introduced.

"Hello," Renate replied, but remained a short distance away as Marek nodded toward her.

Klaus continued, "I need someone to get things started bright and early at 4:30, working for four hours until 8:30. And I might as well be right up-front about it—the job doesn't pay much."

Renate cast a darting look at Marek's reaction and then glanced at her husband. Both their countenances remained straight-faced.

"So you're originally from Poland, right?" Klaus asked. He no doubt wanted to move from the topic of money right away. "I'd like to see your identification papers."

Marek handed them over while he rubbed his chin with his other hand. It appeared he, too, wanted to move off-topic, as he asked, "What kinds of recipes do you use here?"

"Come to the kitchen, and I'll show you," Klaus said. "I would expect you to have some good ones of your own too." As they walked, Klaus examined Marek's papers.

Renate had heard and seen enough. She followed them into the kitchen. "Klaus, what is this all about?"

He turned toward her and winced. "I'll explain later, dear," he said. He sounded like Willy might sound if caught with his hand in the cookie jar.

As Renate caught up to them in the kitchen, Klaus released a barrage of rapid-fire questions about baking which Marek fielded well, sounding more confident with each one—all except the one about references.

He has no references? Renate thought.

Klaus sat down with Marek at a small table, and together

they reviewed recipes in the file. In the background, the radio, the *Volksempfänger* (People's Receiver), provided a war update: "The Army High Command reports that American aircraft suffered significant casualties over the naval port of Kiel."

Fifteen minutes passed, and the interview ended. "Please go home and bake something special," Klaus said. "Bring it here at this time tomorrow morning. The best way to earn this job would be to impress me."

"Yes, sir," Marek replied.

Renate studied Marek's demeanor, the look in his eyes, as though he already had something special in mind. He stood then, without another word, and walked toward the kitchen door, his arms swinging with utmost confidence at his sides. At the door, he turned and looked at Klaus. "Meet you here at 8:30 tomorrow morning."

"Impress me," Klaus replied.

"Klaus, what are you up to?" Renate asked. "I don't like not being a part of decisions like this." She trailed on his heels as he headed to the front room.

"Well, dear, I did plan to discuss this with you. I didn't expect to see an applicant so soon. But if I had asked you earlier, you'd have said no. This way you get to actually meet someone. I think we need some help in the early morning hours doing the baking. It's far too hard on you and Liddy."

"Did I hear my name?" Liddy joined the conversation from the bottom of the stairs.

"Your father wants to hire a young man to help us early in the morning." Renate scowled in disapproval and hoped Liddy would see it as she entered the room. Her scowl deepened upon observing Liddy's face brighten.

"Oh, that would be great, Father. But how is it that we can afford that?"

"I wouldn't pay him much," Klaus said. "There are plenty of refugees keeping wages low. I think we should try it out for a week or two and see how it goes. What have we got to lose?"

****

The next morning, Marek cradled his "baby," his prized loaf of marble rye bread, wrapped with care in brown paper, but that didn't slow down his brisk stride. The bus had been late, and he knew that punctuality was important to employers.

He glanced at his watch and saw he had a minute or two to spare. The fresh aromas that greeted him as he walked through the bakery's doorway convinced him these people knew what they were doing. Would they like what he had to offer?

"*Guten morgen, Herr* Mittendorf," he greeted Klaus, who seemed busy with a broom at the end of his arm.

"*Guten morgen* to you, Marek." Klaus set his broom aside and focused on the wrapped bundle. "I gather you have something to share there."

"This is my specialty—marble rye." He unwrapped the package with great care. "How do you like the looks of this?"

Klaus gazed down at a unique loaf of bread. Inscribed on the top was a scripted letter *M* in dark brown with a long flourish to the right.

"How did you do that?" Klaus asked. "That letter jumps right out at you. What does it stand for anyway?"

"Whatever you want it to," Marek replied, newfound confidence making him more at ease.

"I know," Klaus said. "This could be our signature loaf. The *M* could stand for Mittendorf. I love it." He called out, "Renate, come take a look at this."

She hobbled over from her corner, where she had been slicing fresh dough.

"That loaf looks pretty, but the real test is how it tastes," she said.

Klaus retrieved a knife and thumbed the edge carefully, no doubt to test for sharpness. He then cut off two pieces, giving one to Renate. They each took a bite, and Marek was pleased to see Klaus chewing in search of every nuance of flavor. A wide smile took over his face when he heard him say, "Very nice." Then, "What do you think, Renate?"

"I've had better," she said. Marek felt his heart skip a beat.

"Oh, come now. Be fair," replied Klaus.

"Well, I will admit it has an excellent texture—not too heavy."

"How do you make that fancy *M* stand out?" Klaus asked Marek again. "I can see how you use the dark dough on top of the light, but …"

"I then take a small sharp knife and do some trimming after it's baked to give it more definition," replied Marek. "It gives me a chance to be both creative and artistic. I'm fortunate that my uncle has a well-stocked kitchen so I could come up with this for you."

Klaus looked toward Renate. He paused a moment but then said the words Marek hoped for: "We will hire you. Everything looks good so far. We're willing to try things out for a week to see how it goes. Let's sit down at the table here to discuss details. It all comes down to you—your success is in your own hands."

Marek glanced at Klaus's smiling face, then shifted to Renate, who gave him a condescending look and just walked away.

Chapter 5

L iddy walked into the kitchen early in the morning and stopped mid-stride, startled to see the new hire, Marek, working alongside her mother. She had forgotten this was his first day.

"Hello," she said shyly as the edges of her mouth turned up with a demure smile. "I'm Liddy." Her soft voice disguised a fluttering in her stomach.

Marek looked up from his large slab of dough, and a widening smile revealed a flash of white teeth. "Hello. Good to meet you this fine morning," he said. He punched the dough with great vigor, almost in cadence with his words.

Caught off guard by his strong personality, Liddy looked down. *Don't just stand here. Think of something to say.* The aroma of freshly baked bread at first distracted her, but then prompted her to speak. "I understand you have quite a background in baking."

"I started in the monastery near Warsaw when I was only twelve. I've learned a lot. And even though it really is work, I've resigned myself to do it to earn a living."

"I wish I could say I was earning something," she mumbled.

As his gaze lingered a moment, Liddy felt him sizing her up. He was probably thinking she looked rather ordinary, but she hoped he saw something more than a fresh innocence coming through— maybe her smile or pleasant personality. Marek's attention went back to the dough as he continued to knead with strong hands, his head bowed.

Liddy sneaked a closer look at his face, a round one with a ruddiness softened by dustings of white flour from the morning's work. Messy dark-brown hair that poked out from his baker's hat complemented his distinct eyebrows and prominent nose. She was tempted to tell him about the flour but dared not.

Again, he looked up, revealing deep-brown eyes, determined yet tired. "I'm going to have to get used to the early hours," he said. "That's for sure."

"I don't think I'll ever get used to them." Liddy giggled. "That's why you haven't seen me until now. We're really glad to have your help."

Liddy's mother began gathering pots and pans. She deposited them with a clang into the sink, where they competed with other pans that already claimed a large share of the space. Meanwhile, Liddy put on her apron and peeked into the oven. "What's in here?" she asked. "Ah, smells like muffins. I love that smell in the morning!"

Mother had just stepped behind the pastry case and looked up at the clock when a man in uniform came into the bakery accompanied by his muzzled German shepherd. The officer had a spring to his step as he strode. He made his way to the glass display case near the far wall.

As Liddy worked, she watched every move the man made, her heart racing in fear.

"Heil Hitler!" The officer greeted Mother with a salute and chin held high.

Mother repeated the greeting but with little more enthusiasm than if she were giving him the time of day. Liddy followed his striking blue eyes as he peered into the case. They were not the kind of eyes that darted back and forth with indecision but rather moved with precision from one item to the next. He was a man of authority, homing in on his desired target.

"That one," he said as he pointed to a square of apple streusel cake. A slight smile of anticipation broadened the narrow lips of his pale face. "I expect it will taste every bit as good as it looks. Do you have any coffee this morning?" He handed over a war ration card as payment.

"Yes, we do," Mother replied. "It's so hard to come by, but we were in luck this week." She poured him a cup, but her arthritic hand made the pour an unsteady one. Under the guise of wiping the top of the display case, Liddy dared to move closer to lend assistance. As Mother handed him the cup, Liddy's eyes fixated on the officer's uniform. It was gray-green wool, with dark-brown collar and cuffs with bright green piping and two shiny silver buttons on each. Sculpted three-point flaps with single buttons adorned front-pleated breast pockets, and a thick, black leather belt showcased a silver rectangular buckle, all constraining a slightly bulging girth, one befitting a fifty-year-old.

"That table over there—that's where I'm going to sit with my dog," the officer said as he pulled on the dog's leash. "My name is Keppler, Conrad Keppler. I'm part of the local *Schutzpolizei*," he said with a voice intended to impress. "I make my rounds with my dog, Max, here. We check shops and make sure there is order in the streets. So, I presume you are the wife of the proprietor?"

"Yes, I am. I'm Renate Mittendorf."

"Ah," said Keppler as he made direct eye contact with her. Mother quickly shifted her glance away. Liddy dared to move closer and sneaked a peek at the officer's service field cap that displayed with prominence the national emblem of a silver-gray spread-winged eagle on top of a swastika with a black background.

He turned to find his table. His tall black boots made a distinctive click on the hardwood floor. Once in his chair, Keppler motioned for his dog to lie at his feet. From a side pocket, he pulled out his watch by its chain to check on the time, followed by some papers from a pocket inside his coat.

A few minutes later, Liddy went into the kitchen and came back with a tray of freshly baked signature loaves of bread. Mother took the tray and filled a rack behind the counter. Liddy placed one of the loaves in the display case. Without even a hint of a smile, Mother nodded toward the officer and motioned for Liddy to grab the coffee pot and offer him a second cup. "More coffee, *mein Herr?*" Liddy asked in a soft voice while she avoided eye contact.

"Yes, this is already getting cold," Keppler replied, his tone harsh. But raising his head, then his eyebrows, his demeanor changed in an instant as he stared into Liddy's eyes and locked on them. The corners of his mouth turned up.

"And who are you?" he asked with authority.

"Oh, I'm Liddy. A daughter here." Hands shaking, she dribbled the coffee beside Keppler's cup but was quick to wipe up the spill with her apron.

"Be careful!" Keppler ordered and slapped his palm on the table.

Shaking from head to foot, Liddy turned and rushed into the kitchen, where her fear released a silent stream of tears.

****

Willy hurried down the stairs and noticed the officer with his dog. He walked with caution toward them.

"May I p-pet your dog, sir?" he asked. The dog's eyes appeared to be locked on him.

A low almost inaudible grunt came from the officer.

Willy just stood … waiting.

Keppler replied at last, "Well, all right, but be careful. He may be skittish with strangers. Steady, Max."

Eyeing the muzzle, Willy now approached the dog with confidence. However, when he reached to pet the dog's head, the shepherd growled. In a flash, as if he'd been caged for hours, the dog leapt to his feet with a fierce snarl. Willy jumped up as well, hitting his head on the edge of the table and backing off with fear draped all over his face. "I told you to be careful," Keppler yelled. "Now stay away from him. Look, you've spilled my coffee!"

Willy scurried toward the kitchen as he rubbed the bump on his head. Mother and Liddy stood by the door.

"Don't be bothering the officer and his dog," Mother admonished him. Willy turned to look back at the dog and noticed Keppler had pulled out his watch and was gathering his things. Brushing a few crumbs off his uniform, the officer took one last bite of streusel cake followed by a gulp of coffee. He wrapped a small piece in a napkin and abruptly arose from his chair and pushed it back in place with authority. He headed toward the door with Max stepping in stride, and in an instant, they were gone.

Just minutes later, Father trudged in, home from his night shift at the Tegel prison. Looking relieved, Mother greeted him, "You look like you've had a rough night."

"I'm doing all right. How did you fare with Marek on his first day? Is he still here?"

"Yes." Mother looked behind her as if to make sure he was still in the kitchen. "He seems to know what he's doing, and he's a good worker. Hard to get to know, though. He won't share much about himself. He grew up in Warsaw and worked in a monastery—that's about all I could get out of him. I have no idea how he ended up here. I don't know, Klaus. It's going to take me a while to trust him."

"How is he in the kitchen with the baking and all that?"

"Seems to be doing all right. I tried a few of the things he made, and they all tasted pretty good."

"Many customers this morning?"

"No, not many. But a stranger came in with his dog. He said his name was Keppler, and he's one of the local *Schutzpolizei*. He sure made us feel uncomfortable."

Liddy, who had come from the kitchen, caught the end of the conversation. "Hi, Father. That's right, I did not appreciate Herr Keppler's steely gaze at all. It sent chills down the back of my neck. My body still shakes just thinking about it."

"You should have seen his dog, Father. He snarled and jumped at me!" Willy added.

"It's been a hectic morning," Mother said. "I need a moment of comfort from God." She looked up and whispered a short prayer.

Then came an extended sigh of relief as she stepped back to examine Klaus from head to toe. "My, you are a sight. I must say, I have to give credit to Keppler for his uniform. It sure looked a lot better than the outfit the prison folks have you wearing."

"Oh, that's not important," Father said. "I'm not trying to impress anyone. Besides, it has some nice pockets in the front … Oh, that reminds me. I have a letter here that I promised to deliver." He pulled it out and looked at the address. "You know, this is over in Charlottenburg. Liddy, could you deliver it for me in the next day or two?"

"Oh, Father, please don't ask me to do that! You know I don't like to go out of the house on errands—not these days, especially to strange neighborhoods. I wouldn't know my way around over there. I'd probably get lost." Liddy thought of her time with her *Grossmutter* in Munich. Going to college would have been a big step out. How did she ever think she could do that?

"She's right, Klaus," Mother said. "I don't like her out there on her own. It's too dangerous."

"I'll never forget the time we got lost last winter," Willy said. "It was so cold."

"Well, I'll have to figure out something else," Father replied. "I promised this prisoner I'd hand-deliver it. The man from Cell 92. I don't even remember his name. He's not your ordinary prisoner, though. He brings calm to the whole place. And what I really like is he prays with anyone who will let him."

"So why don't they let him mail the letter?" Mother asked.

"He only gets to send a limited number. Besides, he's a political prisoner, and they read every letter he sends."

"Except this one?" Liddy asked.

"Yes, he sent this one to his fiancée." Father looked again at the front of the envelope. "*Fräulein* Maria von Wedemeyer."

"It sounds like you're taking a huge risk doing this!" Mother's tone clearly indicated she was not happy with this new bit of information. "Klaus, I thought you were taking this job to earn more money and stay on the good side of the authorities. What in the world are you thinking? Have you lost all your senses?"

"Settle down, dear. No need to get all worked up." He paused then let out a huge sigh. "Well, I don't know. I mean … it seemed like the right thing to do." He paused again. "What's wrong with a man sending a few private letters to his fiancée anyway?"

Chapter 6

"Please identify yourself," came the stern voice from the woman behind the massive door.

"This is Marek Menkowicz." As the twilight fast turned to darkness, the woman had little chance to see anyone well through the small security hole. This was made even more difficult with the outside light off.

"Step in," she said.

Without delay, Marek passed through the doorway.

Frau Johanna Solf looked skeptical as she stared at him. Marek shifted uncomfortably on his feet. He released a subtle sigh of relief when the look on her face disappeared.

"Good to meet you." She shook his hand. "Please wait here a moment."

Marek waited in the entryway. He couldn't help but wonder if he had made the right decision to come. He rubbed the back of his neck. What was a seventeen-year-old boy from Warsaw doing in the home of wealthy people in the Wannsee district? He glanced toward the large room off the foyer where *Frau* Solf checked that the dark curtains on each window were pulled tight—no doubt in compliance with government regulations. She then turned on a small lamp.

"Please make yourself comfortable." She gestured toward a soft-cushioned chair with a classy green plaid fabric. "You come highly recommended by *Herr* Rosenberg. So, I understand you fled Poland when things really took a turn for the worse."

"That's right." Marek gazed into space, his mind haunted by visions of the horrors he'd left behind. "It was terrible," he said. He struggled to bring his focus back to *Frau* Solf.

"You look awfully young, though. How old are you?"

"Seventeen. B-But, yes, people have often said I have a baby face."

"Well, let's get down to business. Do you have the samples?"

Marek pulled some pamphlets and leaflets along with false identity documentation out of his rucksack and handed them over.

Frau Solf reached for her purse. "I need to find my reading glasses," she said.

While she rummaged, Marek scanned the room. It was a large living area with several side chairs, a commodious sofa, and a love seat—all arranged around a distinctive beige-brick fireplace. Some folding chairs were still set up and looked out of place among the other pieces of large furniture. Lamps with beautifully ornate shades sat atop side tables with sculpted wood legs, whose polish reflected the meager light cast by the single illuminated lamp.

Marek's breathing became ragged when he felt the eyes of a number of people staring at him from behind. How had he not noticed them come into the room? Dare he turn around and look? Deciding at last to glance back, he felt foolish but relieved to see only a wall full of pictures. *But who were they? What role did they play in Frau Solf's life?*

Frau Solf had moved closer to the lamp to take a better look at the samples. She scrutinized them, in Marek's opinion, like they were diamonds she wanted to purchase. "The pamphlets look good," she said, but before Marek had a chance to react, she added, "I'm afraid a trained eye might pick up on the false identification papers. You'll have to do a better job with them."

Marek's head lowered as he thought how he had rushed through preparation of the papers. "I'll spend more time getting the next group done to your satisfaction. Don't worry."

Frau Solf set her reading glasses softly on the table and got up to walk toward him, her face draped with worry. She stopped in front of him. For a moment, she appeared to be a lioness about to pounce on her prey—at least more than a nurturing mother ensuring that her cub toed the line.

Marek looked away and squirmed in his chair, trying hard to steady his legs.

"Look me straight in the eye, young man," *Frau* Solf said. "This is an extremely serious business. Your success—I should say, our success—is totally dependent on where your heart lies. I pride myself on being a good judge of character. Convince me that I am."

Marek wiped his hand across his forehead, which now glistened with sweat. Regaining his composure, he looked straight into her piercing dark-brown eyes. "I'm not quite sure what to say. But believe me, *Frau* Solf, you can trust me. I will do whatever you need me to do. Let's just say I'm anxious to pay back the Nazis for what happened to my parents and my best friend in Warsaw." His voice was halting, yet he hoped she could tell he was sincere. "There's no reason whatsoever for you to worry about me."

Frau Solf paused. Then, as the lioness again, she slowly circled his chair. "Why should I trust you?" She paused again. "I suppose because I know that Rosenberg has never let me down before. He told me about your parents. I do know that what you're choosing—to do what's right for precious family members—is important. It's a powerful driver.

"But I do believe you," she concluded. "And I'm sure you're well aware that if you're not fully on board, there could be consequences for us all. Have you heard of the counter student group called White Rose down in Munich? In February, they were deemed guilty by the People's Court and executed as traitors."

Frau Solf stroked her hair, then fingered a number of loose strands.

Marek contemplated the magnitude of what she had just shared and how her thin body appeared to bend under the stresses of this kind of thing. Her shoulders, as well, seemed to droop under an enormous weight.

"Well," Frau Solf said, finally shrugging those shoulders. "Our group is not as radical as theirs. We're not into subversion for one thing. We're just a group of serious thinkers concerned about the future of Germany." Her eyes looked distant. "We want fair treatment for all, including POWs and Jews. But we can't forget the possible consequences. We must all be vigilant—there's no doubt about that."

Frau Solf stepped back a few steps and, in deep thought, grasped her chin. "I'll have to let you know when we want to proceed. Here, take these write-ups so you're ready." She handed Marek a folder. "How much notice do you need?"

"Only a few days, *Frau* Solf." Marek stood, put the folder into his rucksack, and prepared to leave. He looked around the spacious room with many fine furnishings one more time. Despite the dim light, he tried to make out the wall full of framed certificates and pictures. One in the center was a large picture of a man, perhaps *Frau* Solf's husband, standing next to another man of Asian nationality.

"That's my husband, Wilhelm, taken when he was the Ambassador to Japan. Wilhelm died several years ago, I am sorry to say. Over on the right is a picture of me with Father Max Metzger. He is a renowned proponent of peace, not to mention ecumenical efforts between Catholics and Protestants."

Marek wasn't sure what "ecumenical" meant, but he knew he felt much better than when he had arrived. In fact, exhilaration now filled his senses. No doubt he was in the company of a person from the accomplished elite—yes, someone with stature, who had similar views about the war.

"This is a very nice place you have here, *Frau* Solf." Marek's eyes widened again. "You've got a lot to be worried about, don't you? Germany is at a critical point."

"Quite the astute observation," she said, then hesitated. A deep furrow formed across her brow. "Yes, indeed, my son. Yes, indeed. We've accomplished a lot in life, but what you see here—they're all just things." She shrugged. "I care more about the future of my country. I care more about humankind." Her teary eyes gleamed.

Frau Solf escorted Marek to the door and looked him straight in the eye as she placed her hands on his shoulders. "I trust we can count on you, Marek," she said. He studied her piercing dark eyes, a look he would long remember. "You'll hear from me through Rosenberg," she said. "Good-bye, and be careful."

Chapter 7

Monday brought a bright sun and warmer temperatures. "How much farther do we have to take this bus?" Liddy asked Marek, the silence now broken.

She gazed out the window and watched people coming and going into stores along the way. She admired how they got on with their busy days and showed no fear, even in the face of a Berlin that was often bombed at night. Munich had seemed safer.

She sat next to Marek, whom she had come to like a lot, and longed to engage in conversation. But why couldn't she be more like other people? Why was she so quiet this fine morning? Quite sure her submissive demeanor had left no favorable impression on him, she stared out the window in disappointment.

"It's only about twelve blocks," Marek replied. "Then we get off and walk four blocks west. Shouldn't be too bad. The way back, though, is another thing. Remember, you promised your father that after we dropped off the letter, we would stop and get more flour and sugar at the dry goods store."

"That's right. I think that's the only reason my mother allowed you to go with me. She's desperate to get the supplies."

"That was quite the verbal battle your parents had. I hope I haven't created any problems. Your mother doesn't really trust me, does she?"

"No, I guess not. But then we don't really know you, do we?" She paused, then asked, "Just what is a young Polish teenager like you doing in Berlin?"

"I fled Warsaw because of what was then going on with the war. Things really got bad. I do have an uncle here who I'm staying with. In the afternoons, I work in the pressroom at the *Die Post* newspaper on the east side of town. I learned all about printing while at the monastery. That's where we printed *The Knight*, which was sent to many countries."

"You've become quite the accomplished tradesman," Liddy said, impressed beyond measure.

"If only your mother would believe that." Marek paused. "I know—maybe if I show her I fully support the Third Reich, she'd feel more comfortable with me. I wonder, do you suppose foreign refugees are allowed to join the Hitler Youth?"

"You would do that?" Liddy looked at him in disbelief. "I've heard that when it comes to enforcement of the law, they can get pretty rough."

"They can be." Marek drew closer and lowered his voice. "I don't agree with some of Hitler's tactics, but I support his efforts to turn Germany into a powerful force the world has to reckon with. Yes, I know he took over my country, but far better the Germans than those bullies to the east, the Russian Communists."

Still in disbelief, Liddy thought about her own family's situation. She didn't know where her parents stood. They had not expressed any strong feelings. She responded at last to Marek, "Well, Mother and Father don't like all this business when they deport the Jews and send them to work camps. But when it really comes down to it, they don't want to get involved. They're focused on survival of the bakery—that's the most important thing. We're all simply striving to get through this war, with hopes for a decent life after it's all over."

Liddy found herself closer to Marek ... able to finally ... freely ... talk to her new friend. Her face ... her heart ... surged with warmth as he stared at her and listened attentively. She looked into his dark brown eyes and wondered if his thoughts were equally as deep. She hoped she had not revealed too much about her parents and was still trying to figure out what he was all about. Suddenly, when Marek reached up to pull the cord to stop the bus, Liddy's train of thought was broken. He gathered up their rucksacks. Liddy reached to make sure her camera was still inside her bag, and they got off.

The four-block walk did not take long, and they soon arrived at the address on the envelope. But no one answered, even after a second and third try. Liddy could not hide her disappointment. Was their trip a failure? She had so looked forward to meeting *Fräulein* Wedemeyer, to see how happy she would be, to describe that look on her face to her father. Now she would have to settle for the letter deposited in the mail receptacle and moving on.

Marek pulled out a map from his rucksack to find their way to the dry goods store. Liddy watched his eyes follow his fingers. She could tell he was no stranger to this well-worn map and admired how deftly he came up with a plan that had them on their way in no time at all. *This would have been impossible for me to do without him*, she reasoned.

Along the way, a vacant storefront caught Liddy's attention. "Look what this war has done. Businesses like this have had to shut down." She looked up at the sign above. Peeling paint revealed that more than one establishment had occupied this space. "Look, Marek. I think I'll get a picture of this."

"You'd want a picture of this broken-down old building with a sign that's peeling?

"Yes, this is history, Marek. Imagine the story behind it. Besides, it is also artistic." She pulled her camera from her rucksack and took several strides at different angles in search of the best shot.

Marek shook his head. "I can only imagine, but then I don't really understand art." He gazed up at the sign. "Say," he said. "Did you notice some of the letters showing through from behind the peeling paint? There's the 'orf' at the end of the first word and the 'itt' near the front. Kind of like your last name. The second word with its 'aur' would indicate 'restaurant' to me.

"Interesting," Liddy replied but was more focused on getting some good pictures.

****

Liddy chuckled at how big Marek's eyes got when he sized up the ten-kilo bag of flour and two-kilo bag of sugar. They had wanted even more sugar, but not unexpectedly, it was being rationed. Nonetheless, to load up everything would be a challenge. Marek sighed from deep within. Liddy held the rucksack open while Marek lifted the flour bag. He lost his grip, the bag hit the ground with a thud, and a slight tear released a small dusting of flour.

"Oh, great." Marek brushed the flour aside and then wiped his brow. He lifted the bag again, and this time, he was able to fit it into the rucksack.

Liddy looked at Marek's "new look" and smiled. With a flour dusting across his forehead and his messy hair, it reminded her of the first day they had met. Now, a new surge of courage empowered her, and she could reveal to him how she felt. She pointed at the flour and laughed as he, embarrassed, jerked back his head—but only a bit. It seemed like he relished her touch.

"I guess you'll do anything you can to show the whole world you're a baker," Liddy said. *And I hope he accepts that as a compliment.*

They arrived back at the bakery late in the morning, the trip uneventful except for lugging the heavy rucksacks. However, once they walked into the Mittendorf establishment, Liddy focused on a sight that tensed every nerve in her body.

Mother lay flat on her back on the floor. Father, in his bathrobe, and Willy hovered over her … along with a stranger.

Chapter 8

"What happened, Father?" Liddy rushed to her mother's side with Marek close behind.

"I think she hit her head," her father said, an ashen pallor draping his face. "I'll bet her knee buckled on her. This is Dr. Reckzeh. It's a good thing he happened to be here. Your brother got me out of bed."

Willy hurried in from the kitchen with a wet cloth and handed it to Dr. Reckzeh. The doctor wiped Mother's face with gentle strokes. "She's got quite a bump on the side where her head must have hit the table. I know ice is hard to come by. You wouldn't happen to have any, would you?"

"I'll check." Willy took off to try to find some.

"Renate, are you all right?" Father asked as he held her hand. "She's going to be all right, Doctor, isn't she?"

"I think so," he said. "Let's see. *Frau* Mittendorf, can you sit up?" He placed his hand behind her shoulder.

"Oh, dear," Mother mumbled. "I don't know what happened. All of a sudden my knee got really weak and gave out on me."

"Perhaps you've been stressed and overtired?" the doctor asked.

"Yes, but it's probably just from my arthritis," she replied.

Dr. Reckzeh and Father helped Mother as she made her way to a chair and slumped down with a loud sigh. Willy returned with some ice, and Liddy wrapped it in the cloth, then held it against her mother's head.

Father gently grasped Mother's hand. "She's a rheumatoid arthritis sufferer, Doctor. She deals with lots of pain all day long." He turned to Liddy. "Did you pick up the aspirin I asked you to get?"

"Oh, Father, I forgot."

"What?" Father's displeasure exuded from his words. "Only three things to do on your trip out, and you forgot one of them?"

"I'm so sorry, Father." She grasped her mother's free hand, then implored, "Mother, please forgive me. You know I'm always thinking of you."

"Don't worry," Dr. Reckzeh said, "I've got something stronger I can give her." He turned to Mother. "This will make you a bit sleepy, but perhaps you should lie down and rest for a while." He reached into his pocket and pulled out a small pill container.

Liddy turned around to look for Marek. She had almost forgotten that he was there.

"Marek, I'm sure you know where the glasses are in the kitchen. Do you mind getting a glass of water for her?"

"Not a problem. But then, so you know, I'll have to head right out to get to my afternoon job."

Father turned to Dr. Reckzeh. "I'm sure you need to get going as well. I can't thank you enough for all you have done." He shook the doctor's hand.

"Well, let me first help get your wife over to the sofa," said the doctor. "I'll stop back sometime next week to check up on her."

"I would much appreciate that."

"After all," the doctor continued, "there are a few items in that pastry case that will bring me back."

Once Mother settled herself and Marek removed the flour bag from his rucksack, he and the doctor left.

Liddy began transferring the flour and sugar into their storage bins.

"Well, at least you picked up the supplies," her father said. "Thank you for that. Did you deliver the letter?"

"Yes, Father, but there was no answer at the door, so we had to leave it in the mail receptacle. It was a beautiful home."

"That's fine," he said. A hint of relief finally showed on a face that had grown weary from the morning's events.

****

Liddy was proud to have prepared a light meal of boiled cabbage, *spätzle* noodles, and a single sausage for everyone to enjoy. However, dinner started without much talk around the table that evening. Mother, in particular, lacked energy and had a glum, expressionless look on her face. Father said a very short prayer of thanks for the food and their family's safety but said little more.

Her demeanor no doubt subdued, Mother spoke after the prayer. "You seem to be going through the motions, Klaus."

Liddy eyed her parents. She could sense the mounting irritation in her mother's voice. "You mean after all we have been through today, you're not going to thank God for my quick recovery—especially for Dr. Reckzeh being here at the right time?"

"Well, I guess I should have. That was an oversight. I'm sorry."

Mother, who could have offered her own prayer of thanks, instead rallied her energy to offer a perceived shortcoming in leadership from her husband. "I wish you would pay more attention to the spiritual needs of this family. In these times, we really need your guidance." She pulled the sausage toward her and began cutting the meat into four pieces, the knife making a sharp sound on the plate, adding more depth to her feelings.

They stared at their food. Occasional forkfuls brought only skimpy amounts to their mouths. Liddy wondered if they were trying to stretch out the meager rations or if they were reacting to her mother's scolding of her father.

At last, Father changed the subject. "We need to discuss the situation with Willy. They're really putting pressure on people to send their kids to KLV camp."

"I've heard of that, Father, but don't like the sounds of it," Willy said with apprehension. "What is it, anyway?"

"It stands for *Kinderlandverschickung*, which is another way of saying 'send your children to the countryside.' They encourage children under the age of fourteen to go away with friends to camps in the country. It's just like going to school, but you would be much safer than staying in the city."

"No, I don't want to go, Father. I'd miss you all. Besides, would they have a piano there?" He grabbed a slice of homemade bread. "Or what about anything like this?"

"We'd miss you too, Willy, but sometimes you have to do what the authorities say," Father said. "You would be with your school friends. We'll just have to see."

"I have mixed feelings," Mother said. "I'd worry so much if he was out of my sight, but then I do want him to be safe."

Liddy sensed that the events of the last few weeks had begun to overwhelm her mother.

Mother continued, "Well, there's plenty for us to worry about these days. For one thing,"—she paused while she chewed slowly on a piece of sausage—"I worry about this fellow, Marek—the one you insisted on hiring, Klaus. How do we know he's not going to get us into trouble? For all we know, he might be Jewish. There, I've said it. Something I've been worried about since he showed up here." Her hand shook as she brought a napkin to her mouth, but the words had already escaped.

"But he comes from a Catholic monastery," Father replied.

"So he says," Mother was quick to add. "But how can we be sure?"

"Well," Liddy said, "I like Marek. I trust him. He sure seems to have our best interests at heart. And he's a hard worker who knows how to bake good things. Have you tried his muffins? They're delicious. And did you know he also works at the newspaper? He's very industrious, you know." Liddy paused to catch her breath. "Mother, everything is going to be all right. You're just out of sorts with what you've gone through."

Without another word, Mother began to gather the dishes. Unlike her regular routine after dinner, the dishes clanged as she stacked them together, and the noise put an end to all further conversation.

Chapter 9

Liddy blamed her curiosity on the aroma wafting from the warm oven. That's what had awakened more than her hunger as she bustled about the bakery that morning. What was the story deep within Marek? She'd been yearning for the past few weeks to figure him out—to get inside his mysterious shell. Liddy had been stuck in her own shell for seventeen years, sometimes feeling trapped and lonely. Marek's shell was unlike her own; he lived outside his. She knew he was a refugee. The cruel war had turned his life upside down, but she could only imagine how horrible it had been. Any details were sketchy at best.

On this particular morning, as Marek's work shift came to an end, she sensed his mind was elsewhere. A casual fling of his apron toward the wall hook left it rumpled on the floor. As Liddy now stood near him in the kitchen, he peeked through the small window of the door to the front room.

"Hurry up—go," he mumbled. He rubbed his forehead back and forth.

"What's going on?" Liddy asked. "Why do you keep looking out that window?"

"I'm trying to leave, but Keppler's still here. Surely you must understand I can never cross paths with that man. A Nazi police officer? Never." Marek fidgeted with his sleeve. Liddy sighed. *That's just it. I want to understand the whole story.*

"Did you park your bike out front?" she asked. "You know *Herr* Kepler has become a regular around here." She hoped her face didn't look condescending.

"I was in a hurry this morning—wasn't thinking. How could I be so foolish?" He looked down and shook his head.

"Well, I have to deal with *Herr* Keppler every day," Liddy added. "Sometimes I just shudder from the tension he creates. Those steely eyes are always watching my every move. The same goes for all the customers who walk in. It's a wonder they keep coming back." She pondered for a moment.

"He's gone. I can leave," Marek said, relief draping his voice. Liddy expected Marek to rush right out. She was thrilled when he turned and gave her a smile and an admiring glance from his deep-set brown eyes. That and his squeeze of her hand set her heart fluttering. If only his touch would last longer. She didn't care that his hand was still sticky from a hurried pass under the faucet.

"See you bright and early tomorrow," he said, already out the kitchen and near the front door.

"What's the rush?" That was a question Liddy knew she'd be asking, now sooner than hoped.

"Nothing—nothing special." Marek's voice hesitated. "Well … I have a printing job at the newspaper. They want me to come in early today." He turned his head to avoid her eyes.

How strange. Liddy knew about his afternoon job at the newspaper, but this would be four hours earlier than normal. Her stomach felt uneasy as she closed the front door behind him. *What's he up to? Won't look straight at me. Seems like he's keeping secrets.* At the front window, Liddy pushed a curtain aside just in time to see Marek retrieve his bike. She chided herself for being so preoccupied with his comings and goings, but engrossed she would remain.

But wait. Instead of heading east toward the newspaper building, he headed west.

Liddy's heart raced. Something about her connection to this mysterious young man was overwhelming. She found her hand pressed to her chest, now tingling with fear. Then came a pull much stronger than fear. Her heart ached, desperate to follow him.

Liddy told her mother she'd be right back and rushed out to get her bike. She knew she'd have a hard time keeping up with him yet wanted to try. She might get lost. She would take the risk. While always pursuing the other half of his story, an overriding fear lingered: she might never find the other half. Until now. This was her chance.

"Marek. Slow down," pleaded Liddy under her breath. What if he looked back and saw her? But she needn't worry. He would never do that. Marek was always looking forward, always moving forward.

Horns blared as she crossed streets. Storefronts were a blur as she whirred by. People scurried to get out of her way, casting angry scowls soon forgotten. But, no, they would not deter her. She pedaled as fast as she could, as a strong breeze whipped her hair. The figure in the distance, however, kept getting smaller. *Please, God, don't let him disappear.*

Fifteen minutes passed, and Liddy was relieved to see Marek pull up to the front of an older building. Window shutters hung crooked, their hinges loose. The dirty brick exterior sat in perfect harmony with the overcast sky. Marek parked his bike close to the building, where nasty weeds had taken full advantage of cracks in the concrete sidewalk. She watched him head up a stairway and through an entry door that had long ago soaked up its last coat of paint.

As Liddy approached the building, a light brought her attention to a window on the lower level. She parked her bike and inched her way to the window. It was narrow, but at eye level. Careful not to touch its weathered sill, laden with slivers, she kept her head low and glanced inside.

Marek was talking to a slender girl with cropped dark hair. When he turned to point in Liddy's direction toward some strange equipment in the room, Liddy ducked. Her heart raced, and she remained hidden as seconds passed. Emboldened at last, she peeked back into the window and gasped. Marek was hugging the girl. Liddy's heart sank so low she might as well have tossed it into one of the street gutters her bike had so easily traversed.

A stern voice from behind startled Liddy. "What are you doing?"

Her stomach churned as she turned around. The older man's stature was as imposing as his voice. A monogrammed oval on his dark blue shirt read *Otto*.

"Oh, nothing, nothing, *mein Herr*," Liddy mumbled. "I just thought I recognized someone inside. It's … an old friend. That's right, an old friend from school … yes, indeed, Otto, *mein Herr*."

"I am Otto Jodmin, custodian of this building. I don't like strangers snooping around here. No one can be trusted these days. I'd better not see you around here again. Now, be off with you."

Liddy scampered to retrieve her bike. She pedaled back home almost as fast as she had come.

****

"So where have you been all this time?" Mother asked with concerned, penetrating eyes. "That's not like you to venture out. Your little brother Willy might be blind to danger, but Liddy, you know what the world is like out there. My head has been spinning with worry." She ran her quivering hand through her gray hair.

Liddy swallowed hard. She didn't like being deceptive, but if her mother's head was already spinning with worry, what would happen if she told her the whole story?

"I went with Marek." Liddy cleared her throat. "He … he thought he had a connection to some supplies that we need for the bakery."

"You mean a black market where people haggle over scarce goods?" An incredulous scowl marked her mother's face.

"Yes, yes, I—I believe so. It turned out to be a dead end, though." *Well, at least the two parts of the story about Marek and the dead end are true.*

"Now, Liddy …"

Here it comes. Liddy had been staring down at her dirty shoes, but now she raised her head and locked her eyes straight on her mother's face. The ever-present deep creases were still there, but the expression of worry seemed to be softening, maybe from the relief of having her daughter in sight. Liddy's spirits began to rise as well. She was, at least, back in familiar territory.

Mother heaved a frustrated sigh, but her tone was firm. "You be careful, young lady. And I mean it. There's so much more about this Marek fellow that we don't know."

Chapter 10

Liddy found herself always defending Marek to her mother. In fact, there may have been a time or two in the kitchen over the past two weeks when he overheard her. Maybe that's why he had asked her to go on a picnic on his day off from his afternoon job at the newspaper.

Flattered beyond words, she found it hard to concentrate on her work, so she planned and schemed to show him her best side.

They decided to go to Tiergarten, a large park close to the center of the city; they would ride their bikes and carry their rucksacks.

Not one to take a leisurely ride, Marek charged ahead until a stoplight or heavy traffic would give Liddy the chance to catch up.

"What's your hurry?" she finally yelled.

"I don't know. I guess it's hard for me to slow down. I only know one speed."

"Well, take a cue from nature. It's the middle of the day, the sun is out, and a gentle breeze caresses our faces. No one would know a war rages on around us."

They found a quiet spot in the park where a large oak tree provided some shade. Liddy pulled out a blanket and spread it on the lush green grass. "See," she said. "Listen to those birds chirping. Certainly, you can relax now."

Marek stroked Liddy's hand. "Yes, thank you. You and nature, you both bring me a sense of calm—except when you panic about something gone wrong in the kitchen."

Liddy laughed. "I didn't panic when I made these sandwiches. They should help settle your hunger pangs. I must admit, though, you won't find much meat between those slabs of marble rye. But then it's *your* bread, and that's the best part, isn't it?"

"Thanks again," Marek replied, a twinkle of appreciation in his eyes.

Liddy continued to unpack and poured apple juice into two cups. In quietness, they ate their sandwiches and gazed at the surroundings. The midsummer green filled their senses, disrupted by few people, the faint noise of passing cars the only thing that disrupted their serenity.

"So tell me," Liddy said, "you've said you're living here with your uncle, and you left Warsaw because of the war unrest. I hope you don't think it forward of me to ask, but did your parents send you away because they thought it would be safer?"

At first, Marek didn't respond. "Not exactly," he finally stammered as he cleared his throat. "I may as well let you know…" He hesitated. "My parents have disappeared. I haven't heard from them in months. I came home one day, and they were gone. Just like that. There was a half-chopped celery stalk in the kitchen and a half-filled teacup on the table. My best friend, Micah, who had been staying with us for a while, disappeared that day as well."

"Oh my! How devastating! What did you do?"

"I tried to find out what happened but couldn't get any answers. At last, after several days, I contacted my uncle who told me to come to Berlin."

Marek reached for his rucksack and fumbled through its contents. "I have a few mementos with me." He pulled out a family photo. "Do you think I look more like my father or my mother?" he asked.

"I would say more like your mother."

"That's what most people say." Next, he retrieved a piece of jewelry. "This was my mother's favorite brooch. She would wear it when she got all dressed up. My parents didn't go out very often, but I can picture her with a smile on her face, ready to spend an evening out with my father."

Liddy studied the brooch with admiration. "Oh, this is so beautiful." Slowly, she shifted her attention from the jewelry to Marek's eyes—eyes that began to well up with emotion. Her own eyes moistened with tears, and Liddy squeezed his hand.

Marek must not have wanted to linger with that emotion, as he directed his attention back to his rucksack. He pulled out a small box with lettering on the outside.

"What in the world is that?" Liddy asked.

"This is called a *mezuzah*. It was on the doorpost of our house. I wanted to bring some remembrance of our home. Inside is a scroll of scripture from Deuteronomy that provides a blessing for the home." Marek smiled. "The lettering on the outside means 'El Shaddai' or 'God Almighty.'"

"I've never seen anything like this. Can I show it to my family?"

"All right, but be careful. This is a very personal thing, so please don't show it to the whole world. I really like it because it was one of our most prized possessions. It came from Micah's family. They gave it to us when we moved into our home, and Mother always said if we ever moved out, we should take it with us."

Liddy packed the *mezuzah* into her rucksack. As she set the rucksack on the blanket, it tipped over. Her glass of juice ended up on its side, and the sticky liquid soon made its way to Marek's pant leg. He lurched backward.

"Ack-k!" he said, as he tried to wipe the juice away.

"Oh, I'm so sorry! I'm so clumsy!" Liddy grabbed a handful of napkins and tossed them at Marek.

"I've got something that will help." Marek reached into his rucksack and pulled out a handkerchief. "Not exactly what it's intended for, but it comes in handy. Something else from my mother. It's monogrammed. I hate to admit it, but I often use it to wipe down my bike."

As Marek worked to soak up the spill, Liddy tried to think of something that would change the focus away from the disruption she had just caused.

"Wh-What about your father? Did you keep something of his?"

"I have a compass." Marek finished wiping his pant leg then pulled the compass out of his rucksack. "But I kept it more so I could use it. It doesn't bring back the best of memories."

"How so?" Liddy asked, her eyes wider.

"My father loved to take us all on hikes in the countryside, and he would always bring this compass. He also constantly bragged that he never got lost."

"What's so bad about that?"

"Well, it's part of a pattern. He always liked to brag about his accomplishments. He was a very successful salesman for a pharmaceutical company. The problem is he didn't let only us know it, but everyone else too. Sometimes it was embarrassing. I really think the aspirins sold themselves."

"Except if I'm the one who is supposed to pick them up for my mother," Liddy added. Then she reflected for a moment. "You speak of your parents in the past tense. That doesn't mean you've given up all hope, does it?"

"Oh, no, no. I'm still praying that God will deliver them." He paused, his eyes glassy, then turning reflective. After a moment, he asked Liddy, "Didn't you bring anything in your rucksack besides food?"

"Oh, all I have is a bunch of photos." She reached for them. "Mostly buildings. Someday I would like to have a book printed up of historical buildings and monuments throughout the country. Here's a few—the Great Hall, the Berlin Palace, and the Kroll Opera House." She handed them over to Marek. "Unfortunately, I lost many of them in a kitchen fire at my *Grossmutter's* in Munich." Liddy gazed off into the distance.

"I may be able to help you. While at work at the newspaper a few days ago, I came across files and files of pictures stored away. It was unbelievable how many there were."

They finished their lunch, and Liddy began to gather their things. While she reached into her bag, she came across something she remembered was important. "Oh, I almost forgot. My father gave me another letter from that pastor at his prison—this time for his parents." She looked at the envelope and read it aloud: "*Herr* and *Frau* Karl Bonhoeffer." Wait, it's the same address we went to before by bus. His fiancé must be living with his parents. Do you suppose we could bike over there?"

"Well, that's a few kilometers west of here—all the way through the park. It's quite a wealthy area. But it would be a beautiful ride. Do you feel like tackling it?"

"Yes, I think so," she said with a determined smile. "But I have an idea. I've been thinking about that sign over that dilapidated storefront. I'm really curious about what was underneath. Could we go a few blocks out of the way and try to scrape off some of the paint? We could take a long stick with us." She looked around. "There's one," she said while pointing. "One more thing, though. You have to promise not to race ahead of me."

Chapter 11

F ive o'clock Friday morning, Marek pulled open a drawer of the desk in the side room of the bakery. The light from the small desk lamp projected poorly into the drawer, and Marek's sleepy eyes struggled to find what he was looking for.

"What are you doing?" Renate's firm voice startled Marek.

"Oh, *guten Morgen, Frau* Mittendorf. I was … looking for some recipes. Willy told me yesterday I might find them here."

"I moved all our recipes to the file drawer in the kitchen a few weeks ago. Why would you rummage in our desk without my permission?"

"Well, I wanted to surprise you with something special—one of your favorites." Marek tried to respond in an upbeat way, to break the tension.

"How would you know what that is?" Renate asked.

Her desire to force the matter caught Marek off guard, but he answered truthfully. "Well, I was going to pick the most worn-out, stain-covered, recipe card."

"We don't have the luxury to experiment, Marek. Key ingredients are too hard to come by." Renate's patience appeared to grow thinner.

"Listen. I don't want you snooping into our things. You must ask first. Please don't let me catch you at it again."

"I won't. I'm very sorry, *Frau* Mittendorf. It won't happen again. I assure you."

****

Later the next morning, Liddy watched *Herr* Keppler come in and settle into his usual chair in the corner with his regular streusel cake. The quiet was soon shattered when he dropped the piece onto the plate and yelled, "*Frau* Mittendorf!"

Mother rushed over, as fast as her cane-assisted gait would allow. "What's the matter, *Herr* Keppler?"

"This streusel cake is awful—it has no taste whatsoever." He smacked his lips together in search of flavor. "And the coffee, I cannot drink it. This is totally unacceptable."

"I'm so sorry, *Herr* Keppler. But because of shortages we've had to cut back on the sugar in our recipes. And the ground coffee we get these days … well, it seems like it's half sawdust. We can't help it. Maybe you'd like to try something else that's not supposed to be so sweet?" She called out to Liddy, "Bring *Herr* Keppler a signature loaf."

Liddy grabbed a signature loaf off the back rack and located a sharp knife. "Just a moment, *Herr* Keppler, I'll cut a couple of slices of this delicious marble rye for you. It's been a popular item for us of late." Once done, she set the plate in front of him with a smile.

Keppler studied the loaf. "Well, that's an interesting piece of work. Anything has got to be an improvement." He took a bite, gave a less-than-enthusiastic nod of approval, and then waved the women away.

However, Liddy, for the first time in his presence, felt a rush of strength envelop her and lingered. "*Herr* Keppler, you've got to admit that tastes pretty good," she dared say.

Keppler glared at her, then spoke with a hint of kindness. "I suppose—I've had worse." He waved her off again and pulled out a large document from inside his coat pocket.

Liddy watched as he unfolded it; a pass of his hand smoothed its creases on the table. It flattened with ease, no doubt not the first time this document had been laid out. Keppler lowered his head to get a closer look, studying a multitude of green blotches on what appeared to be a map. In search of an excuse to ask him about it, Liddy fetched the coffee pot.

"*Herr* Keppler. I'll pour you a fresh cup." As she filled the cup, she studied the map and said, "That looks like a very interesting map. May I ask what all those green spots represent?"

"They're troop deployments, *Fräulein*."

His cold response did not deter her. "So you know about where our troops are deployed? I guess I shouldn't even be looking at it."

"It's not this war. It's from the last war." The tone of Keppler's voice was even more welcoming, and Liddy sensed that he was pleased she had taken an interest. "This is a map of the battle where my brother suffered serious injuries." Keppler spoke with deep emotion and moved uneasily in his chair.

"So why do you study it?"

"To see how the military leaders made some critical strategic errors. We learn from history. We learn from our mistakes. Look over here at the right. Without a doubt, they left the right flank undermanned. Never leave your right flank exposed, *Fräulein*." He paused and stared up at her. The look on his face portrayed his sincerity in trying to tell her that the magnitude of this gem of wisdom should not go unnoticed. "My brother never recovered."

"Oh, I'm so sorry."

A noise in the side room distracted Liddy, and she turned in that direction. Willy had made his way to the piano for his morning practice. As he started to play the German national anthem, Keppler's ears perked up. Hearing the melody of the first stanza of "*Das Deutschlandlied*," he declared, "What a glorious melody. Haydn surely did an exquisite job when he composed that. *Deutschland über alles—*"

But then as any child would, Willy stumbled over a number of notes.

The officer's sense of well-being shattered. His demeanor changed as his face turned redder with each miscue. "Rubbish!" he yelled as he pounded the table. "Can't you people here get anything right this morning?"

Keppler shoved away from the table and stomped toward the piano, Max close behind at the end of his leash. Although Willy continued to play on, the clicking of Keppler's boots on the floor drowned out his notes—which Liddy guessed was intentional.

"That isn't how you play it!" Keppler said. "I'll show you the right way." With a brusque wave of his hand, he motioned for Willy to move over on the piano bench. "Look," he said. "This is how your fingers need to move for this part." He played the stanza and repeated it several times … perfectly.

Willy sat enthralled with the mastery of Keppler's strokes yet not daring to say a word.

"Here. Now you do it," Keppler said.

Willy tried, and although much improved, failed to meet Keppler's demands.

"This is our national anthem, young man," Keppler declared. "You must honor it—respect it. You must work on it until you've mastered it. Many a brave German soldier has died with the echoes of its melody in his head."

"Yes, *mein Herr*," Willy responded, biting his bottom lip.

Liddy approached the officer. "But did you know, *Herr* Keppler, that *Deutschland über alles* wasn't intended to mean Germany over all the world? It was a rallying cry to bring the independent German states together. I learned that in school."

Keppler turned toward Liddy. His face flushed again with a scowl. This intrusion into his area of expertise had made things worse. With a glare, he said, "Well, that was one misguided teacher!" He yanked on the chain of his watch as he stood to tower over Willy. "Oh, I've got to get going." More harsh words seemed to be at the tip of his tongue, but then his shoulders relaxed. In a measured tone, he proceeded, "Next time, I trust you'll play this much better. It deserves much better." The officer pulled on his dog's leash. "Come, Max. We've spent far too much time at the Mittendorf Bakery this morning."

Liddy made one last attempt to smooth things over before he left. "*Herr* Keppler, these are difficult times for everyone. You've got to be more patient with us here." *Under this man's gruff exterior there has to be a more sensitive man. There just has to be*, she reasoned.

He gave her a disgruntled look. "*Fräulein*, let me decide how patient I should be. That is none of your business." He turned, clicking his heels with authority, and stormed out.

"Have a good day," Liddy called after him, but he had already disappeared from view.

****

Liddy sat with her father in his bedroom as they listened to the British Broadcasting Corporation on the radio late that evening. The bedroom and the kitchen were the only places they dared to hear the faint news, as it had been declared a crime to listen to foreign radio. She yearned to go to her comfortable bed but was intrigued by the latest information. Her father stood up in front of the mirror to check his hair and uniform before heading off to work.

The voice on the radio reported, "Fresh off their victories over the Axis troops in Northern Africa, British General Montgomery and U.S. General Patton have quickly led over half a million troops across the island of Sicily."

Yes, life is so very difficult here during this horrible war, Liddy lamented, *yet how much harder it must be for the soldiers.*

The reporter continued, "Many German and Italian soldiers have escaped across the Strait of Messina to the mainland. What lies ahead for the Allies? They may be intent to march north through Italy to gain control. Mussolini has been deposed in Rome."

Liddy had heard enough about the war. "Father, could I ask you a question?" She scratched her elbow.

"This sounds important." He moved to turn the radio off. "What is it, Liddy?"

"Do you know anything about a 'Mittendorf Restaurant'?"

Her father's head raised abruptly. "How is it you know about that?" The pitch in his voice got higher.

"When Marek and I were out and about a while back, we ran across this broken-down old building. We scraped the paint off an old sign above the door. Underneath it said: 'Mittendorf Restaurant.'"

"That was your *Grossvater's* business." He rubbed the back of his neck.

"How come I never knew anything about it?"

"Your *Grossvater* didn't want anyone to know about it. He was too embarrassed."

"Can you talk to me about it? I would really like to know." She tilted her body forward.

"Well, it failed. They went bankrupt. That's about all I can say. It's one of the reasons your *Grossvater* moved to Munich. To get away from the bad memories."

Her father stood up to leave for work. It seemed that was all he wanted to say about *Grossvater's* failure.

****

The siren wailed long and loud, piercing the quiet of the predawn dark. At 4:30 Monday morning, Marek had just arrived at the bakery, ready to get hard to work. But the siren changed his plans in a heartbeat.

Still in her bathrobe when she greeted Marek, Liddy blushed with embarrassment when his stare drifted from her head to her toes. Thankful that darkness filled the room, she turned in haste to join her family as they scrambled to secure the house.

Liddy rushed to open the windows. That was part of the government-recommended procedure.

"Hurry! Get down in the cellar," yelled Mother to Willy, who dashed into the kitchen from upstairs.

"What can I do?" Marek asked.

"Go down into the cellar and shut off the water and electricity," Mother said. The light from her flashlight bounced around the room like the frenzy in her voice.

The walls shook as the force of a bomb left no doubt it had struck nearby.

"Is a bomb going to hit our house? Is a bomb going to hit our house?" Willy repeated in a shrill voice.

"I don't think so. Don't worry," Liddy tried to reassure him but conceded to herself her words sounded hollow with a lack of conviction. She followed Marek and Willy downstairs.

In the cellar, Willy helped find another flashlight for Marek, who managed to shut off the utilities. Liddy looked up the stairway and spotted her mother at the top. The beam of light from Liddy's flashlight caught the fear on her mother's face as she struggled to keep herself propped up with her cane.

"Take it easy, Mother. Go slow." Liddy raced up the stairs and steadied her mother as she took her flashlight.

"I can't make it down these stairs anymore," she cried. "They're too steep. I know I'll tumble head over heels. What am I going to do? Oh, God, help me!"

Chapter 12

"Fear not, *Frau* Mittendorf! God willing, we're going to get you down these stairs," Marek assured her as he made his way up the stairs and to her side.

The force from another bomb rattled dishes in the cupboards. A sudden shattering of glass made everyone flinch. Liddy pointed her flashlight toward the noise in the front room. A picture of *Grossmutter* and *Grossvater* had fallen to the floor.

"Hurry, we must get downstairs," Mother pleaded.

Liddy clutched her mother's arm. "Marek, this stairway is too narrow for us to go down side by side."

"I've got an idea," Marek said. "I'll carry your mother."

"Marek, you're not that big," Liddy objected. "How are you going to do that?"

"I think if I go down backward and keep my center of gravity low—that should work. Liddy, squeeze past me and go ahead of us. Trust me, *Frau* Mittendorf—we're going to get you down. You've got to trust us. Really, you must."

"Don't worry, Mother." Liddy nodded encouragement to her mother. "You'll be fine."

"Are you ready?" Marek asked.

When Mother hesitated, Marek assured her, "We have no time. Put your arms around my neck … Hurry." He was tender as he cradled the woman in his arms.

As gently as Marek moved, Mother gasped in pain.

"Easy, Marek. Be careful."

"Sorry," he said. "I am trying to be careful."

They headed down the stairs. Liddy supported Marek's back as a precaution and lit the way. Step by step, the wooden planks creaked beneath them under the shifting load, interrupted by the sounds of more bombs that exploded in the distance. At last at the bottom, Marek breathed deep and labored to catch his breath.

"Praise God," said Mother. Her heavy breaths cut short any further speech as Marek eased her body onto a bench in the corner.

Liddy sighed in relief. She reached for her mother's hand and tried to comfort her.

The siren had long since stopped, but the noise from strikes nearby continued.

"Let's say a prayer," Mother said, now settled, but her breathing still deep and jagged.

The others circled around her and joined hands as she led them with an earnest plea for God's protection. "Father God, though we tremble here in fear …"

The words echoed in Liddy's mind from other such trips to the cellar.

"… we know that you are the source of the comfort we need. Keep us safe …"

The prayer brought them a sense of peace with a quiet lull afterward. Marek looked over to check on Mother. "It must have been a while since you've been down here. I'll bet those stairs looked pretty scary."

"Yes, I'm used to sending Willy or Liddy down to get what I need. But it's hard to believe my mobility has taken such a turn for the worse." She shook her head. "Believe me, having arthritis and getting old is disheartening, to say the least."

"It's got to be tough to deal with—so hard to keep your spirits up," Marek said. "Maybe some of it's from stress. We'll keep praying for you—that's for sure. And whenever I'm here, just yell when you need help."

A new impact caused bits of dirt and dust to cascade down. Marek studied the timbers that supported the ceiling. "Looks like Klaus recently reinforced these. I think they'll be fine."

"Father … I wonder how he's doing at the prison," Willy said.

"We can only hope and pray for the best," Mother said.

"We're resilient people," Marek added. "We'll all recover and get on with our lives."

"Faith in God is what will get folks through this ordeal," Mother replied.

Liddy thought about the shattered picture of her grandparents upstairs. Yes, it was only a photograph, but it was like the jagged edges of the glass shards were now piercing the very fabric of her soul. *No, I won't stand for this,* she told herself. *This isn't the way it's supposed to be. I wish Father were here. I worry about Grossvater and Grossmutter in Munich. Families shouldn't be shaking with fear, huddled in cellars.* Her shoulders shuddered; she longed to be in the firm embrace of her father's arms. Her hands were cold and clammy, her stomach hollow. She tried to imagine something warm like freshly baked bread pulled from the oven. Tears slowly trickled down her cheeks, and she longed for *Grossmutter's* cat to lick them away. Fear— it was horrible. A series of loud explosions outside startled Liddy out of her trance. She jumped up, wide-eyed with terror.

Marek reached to squeeze her hand. "Try to relax, Liddy."

But her breathing remained labored. "My mind keeps racing. I worry about my family and friends. I keep imagining all the destruction around us. When, oh when, will the all-clear siren go off?"

At last, in exasperation she yelled, "Please, God. Enough of this war!"

****

After the all-clear siren, Liddy, Willy, Marek, and Mother climbed upstairs. For Mother, the trek up the stairs was much easier. After they cleaned up the worst of the messes, Liddy and Marek ventured outside. The rising sun revealed little about what was directly in front of them. Dark and mysterious, a gaping hole the size of a small car had gouged out the street right in front of the bakery. Liddy peered in but could see nothing but crumbled pavement and smoke.

"It's a good thing that one didn't hit a house," Marek said.

"Those bombers—why don't they just leave us alone?" Liddy cried as she stood by Marek's side. He gazed up as if in search of more planes.

The steady wind pressed hard against their faces—somber faces that eerily mirrored each other as they took in the depth and breadth of the destruction. Fortunately, the immediate surroundings of the bakery were not damaged, but about half a block away, many of the structures had walls tumbled down, windows shattered, bricks strewn about, and rubble everywhere—some tossed aside by people who scurried about with desperate eyes in hunt of precious possessions. Liddy prayed they were not searching for loved ones. Others sat with forlorn faces, still in a state of shock. Liddy and Marek started to head back.

"When I see this, my heart goes out to all the displaced families," Liddy said. "There's got to be a lot of people who are desperate for help." Her eyes widened as she thought further. "That reminds me—it's a good thing we have a clothing drive going on at my church this weekend. Marek, we could sure use some help with those heavy boxes. There are so few men around. You don't suppose you could lend a hand this Saturday afternoon at my church? The way you lifted my mother like she was just another sack of flour, you should have no problem moving a few heavy boxes around."

"Oh, I'm sorry. Saturday afternoon doesn't work for me," Marek said. "I have another commitment with *Frau* Solf. I'm sorry—I'd be happy to help you some other time."

Liddy glanced away. *Who was this Frau Solf?* She knew there was no way to mask her disappointment. Marek continued to puzzle her. Since following him on her bicycle that day to the apartment building, Liddy remained confused about him and what seemed like his buried secrets. "That's the only time the whole group is organized to get together," she said sternly. "And with this bombing, chances are there will be a big turnout."

"I'm sorry, Liddy. I can't."

"We'll see—maybe there'll be another Saturday," she responded. To say that was one thing, but—truth be told—her effort to be polite would not make it any better. *Can't Marek see how important this is to me?* It was such a critical cause vital to the community—especially after a horrible air raid. She, with the tender heart, wanted to put clothes on people over just about anything else. *But why would he make Frau Solf more important than me ... or helping others?*

They returned to the bakery and found Mother still picking up the items that had fallen from shelves. Willy held the dustpan as she swept broken glass from the picture frame.

"I so adore this picture of your father's parents," she said. "Well, at least the picture isn't ruined. We can always get a new frame. But maybe that will have to wait until after the war. So, how does it look outside?"

"You wouldn't believe the size of the hole we found out in the street," Liddy said. "There's a lot of damage to buildings not far from us. We are truly blessed we did not have some of that kind of destruction." Liddy reflected for a moment. "It's a war zone—need I say more?"

****

Several days later as the Mittendorf family sat around the dinner table, a somber mood still had its unrelenting grip on everyone. Liddy studied her brother's face strained with fear as he watched his parents stare at each other and then at him. Neither Father nor Mother appeared ready to say what apparently needed to be said.

"Will you pass the *spätzle*, Liddy?" Mother asked.

Finally, Father spoke. "Willy, considering how dangerous it is here, I think this idea of going to KLV camp is probably the best thing."

"No! I don't want to go!" Willy folded his arms as his eyes filled with tears. "Please don't make me. I'll be safe—don't worry. I'll always be the first one into the cellar. I promise. Please?"

Mother put her arm around him. "I'm very sad about it too, Willy. Sometimes we have to do things we don't like to do," she said in a comforting voice. "You'll be much safer in the country," she assured him. "You've got a great future ahead of you after this horrible war."

"When would I have to go?" Willy swallowed, as the muscles of his neck tensed up.

"We'll have to check with the authorities, but probably soon," Father replied.

Willy, his face glum, picked at his *spätzle,* then pushed it to a different spot on his plate.

"I know it's a sad turn of events," Father said, "but this is a time of sacrifice. Despite all we have been through lately, we really are blessed. What if I had to go fight on the frontline, for one thing? Or just imagine if I were one of the prisoners at the jail." He chewed slowly, as he appeared to pull his thoughts together. "I asked my pastor prisoner today how he copes with all he has been through. You know they are holding him for his plot to kill Hitler. He said that it is only by living completely for God in this world that we learn to have faith."

Oh, no—we're not going to get a lecture, are we? Liddy thought. Then she remembered that Father often quoted someone else when that person made an impression on him. Father continued, "By experiencing life's duties, problems, successes, and failures, we throw ourselves completely into the arms of God—we focus not on our own suffering but on others' troubles in this world."

Liddy wondered if Willy had understood any of Father's wise words because he had a puzzled look on his face. Then she gazed at her mother, whose eyes were fixated on her husband with a look of admiration.

"Klaus," Mother said. "That really brings some perspective to what we are going through. Thank you for sharing that."

"What's more," Father added, "according to *Herr* Bonhoeffer, our happiness can't depend on our circumstances—it's all about what's inside a person."

"Well, the Lord knows if it's just circumstances, it would be tough to be happy in this world," Mother replied. "With or without a war."

Liddy figured her mother had summed it up quite well.

Chapter 13

"See? Doesn't it feel good to sit here for a moment and relax?" Dr. Reckzeh sat at a table in the bakery with Mother. From behind the counter, Liddy caught a beaming smile on her mother's face.

"Yes, but I feel so guilty if I'm not doing something," Mother replied.

It occurred to Liddy that the attention from the doctor must have been stronger than Mother's guilt.

"You've got to get over that and listen to your body. Get off your feet from time to time," Dr. Reckzeh said.

"I'm going to try. I certainly appreciate your stopping by to check on me."

He took a large bite of his pastry. "Well, you know why I'm really here," he said in a whimsical tone as he gestured toward his mouth.

"I'm glad that you like our pastries, Dr. Reckzeh. You know what it's been like with all the bombing. If you only knew how hard it has been on us. It was a nightmare for me to get down into the cellar during the air raid the other night." She shook her head in earnest.

"I certainly admire your fortitude during these trying times. And considering what you've been through, you look well."

"Thank you, Doctor. You've been so good to me." She smiled.

The doctor wiped his mouth with a napkin, stood, and pushed his chair in. "Well, I've got a busy day ahead of me, so I must be off. Good-bye and have a good day," he said, then left.

Liddy stood in fond admiration of her mother. "Mother, you look relaxed for a change."

"Yes, I'm doing much better. I've recovered from the last few stressful days. As Pastor Bonhoeffer pointed out, I try not to let circumstances control my mood."

"Well, then perhaps it's a good time to ask you."

"Oh, no. I don't like the sound of that. Ask me what?"

She could not get it out fast enough. "Marek asked me to a dance." She gave Mother her best smile. "Hopefully, you're feeling better about him after what he did during the air raid."

"A dance? I didn't know there was such a thing these days. Where is it?"

"At Pharus Hall in the district of Wedding. It's not that far away."

"Well, I don't know. There's an air-raid shelter nearby, right?"

"I'm pretty sure there is."

"What kind of music do they play?"

"I'm not sure. Are you saying I can go find out?" Liddy asked, in hopes of a positive response.

"My mind is telling me no, but my heart is saying yes. You're starting to like this Marek fellow, aren't you? You wouldn't be out too late, would you? Do you promise to be extremely careful?"

"Of course, Mother. Marek knows his way around. He knows what he's doing."

"Well, you were right," her mother sighed. "The Lord knows you caught me at a good time. You deserve to have some fun." After a short pause, Mother said, "Well, for a change, *I'll* be the one talking your father into this."

"I just know Father will say it's all right." *At least, I hope he does.*

****

Liddy often gazed at the moon out of her bedroom window on calm nights. She noticed that whatever the moon lacked in fullness, it made up for in brightness. But that was only when the shrouds of gray clouds got out of the way, and a strong wind often tried to make that happen.

The evening Liddy and Marek went to the dance, wisps of gray streaked by in front of the moon, and bright yellow beams of light flashed, then disappeared. As Liddy and Marek approached the entrance to Pharus Hall, she wondered if that wasn't like her relationship with him—flashes of interest followed by darkness. At least she knew the moon was always there. She hoped the same would be true for Marek.

Inside the hall, Liddy couldn't believe the number of youths that had gathered to dance. She guessed well over a hundred. "So, have you been here before?" she asked Marek.

"Oh, a few times. I really like the swing music they play in some of the back rooms. A fellow by the name of Manfred Omankowsky is often here. He's considered the leader of the 'Swing Kids.'"

They walked into a crowded room, and right away other dancing youths jostled them about. Like raisins thrown into a mixing bowl of batter, Liddy felt they had no choice but to get enmeshed. It was an exciting new social scene. Great music played but soft enough that conversations could be overheard.

Liddy's ears picked up some distinct anti-Nazi talk. "Sounds like this is a political group," she said.

"Yes, it can get that way," Marek said. "Fine by me, but I focus on the music. Come on. Let's dance." He grabbed her hand and spun her so their arms were fully extended. He pulled her back and twirled her all the way around. They danced until the fast music stopped.

The band started a slow song, and Marek pulled Liddy close.

She felt a rush of emotions well up through her body. Her hands perspired, and the back of her neck tingled. For a moment, all the worldly cares of war vanished.

Again, the music stopped, but Liddy's heart kept racing. "That was nice," Marek whispered in her ear. "Don't you wish we could do this more often?"

"I sure do," she replied as Marek held her close, peaceful and content.

For some time—Liddy hoped it would be forever—they danced, then suddenly a commotion stirred at the main entrance.

"What's going on?" Liddy asked. She sensed this was no minor disruption.

"Oh, no," Marek said. "It's the Hitler Youth. They can be really nasty. We've got to get out of here fast." He grabbed her hand and pulled her toward a back entrance, where many of the others jammed together in search of a way out.

"It looks like one of the doors must be stuck," Marek said.

Liddy looked back in horror as the Hitler Youth pushed forward. Their clubs swung wildly in every direction. "Help us, dear God," she prayed, her words squelched by the din of screaming around them.

Marek pushed into the crowd harder, trying to find a way out. On the dancers' heels, the Hitler Youth beat anyone in their way.

As Marek and Liddy pushed, the door sprang open, and like apples from a bag that had suddenly burst, bodies tumbled outside.

"Let's get away from here!" Marek helped Liddy up from the ground. "Hurry!"

A Hitler Youth came rushing out the door and tackled Liddy.

"Help, Marek!" she screamed.

Marek turned and grabbed the arms of the youth, wrestling him to the ground. An elbow thrust backward caught Marek square in the chest and sent him reeling onto his back. The lumbering youth staggered to his feet in time to charge Marek. Marek jumped up, and they stared at each other with determined faces.

"Get out of here. Run!" he yelled at Liddy. She moved farther away but couldn't force herself to leave.

Marek bounced back and forth on his feet, feigning darting charges, then thrust his shoulder into his assailant's stomach, knocking him to the ground in a heap. Marek leaned over him, then landed a mighty swing to his jaw. He turned, spotted Liddy, and ran toward her. "Keep going! Don't stop, Liddy." He ran to her side, and they took off running.

"Are you all right?" she asked.

"I-I think I'm okay," he gasped as they hurried down a dark street. A light rain had begun to fall, but getting wet was the least of their worries. Marek looked back. The Hitler Youth, now on his feet, began to pursue but slipped on the wet pavement and fell.

"Quick, let's turn down this alley," Marek said. They abruptly changed directions, and rounding the corner, there was a flash of light when a door opened as a man put out the garbage.

"Please, sir," Marek said. "Can we come in?"

The couple rushed by him, and, as soon as the man stepped inside, Marek slammed the door shut.

"Where are we?" Marek asked while he massaged his right hand.

"Beck's Café," said the man. His jaw still hung, bewildered.

"That's what I thought. Well, I think we'd like a soda," Marek's nonchalance surprised Liddy.

The man, possibly a waiter, anchored his hands on his hips and laughed. "Well, if you want to order something, you came in the wrong door. Just walk right through that doorway." He pointed to another room several feet away. "I must get back to work, so you two just make your way into the café."

"Thank you," Marek said then turned to Liddy. "How about you? Hope you're not too shaken up."

Still trying to catch her breath, Liddy said, "I'm fine. Maybe a slight scrape here." She checked her elbow. "But don't worry about me."

"Well, I did something to my right hand when I took a swing at that fellow. It really hurts." He gently rubbed his hand.

"I hope it's nothing serious. That was a close call." She paused and looked at Marek in amazement. "Now don't tell me you knew about this place."

"Of course I did," he replied with a wink. "I knew there was a café somewhere over in this direction." He gently brushed aside strands of wet hair that clung to her cheeks.

"I must look a fright," she said.

He pulled her closer. "No. I'm looking at a beautiful vibrant face—fresh and sparkling. Your inner beauty always comes through for me—no matter what's happened. Let's sit here awhile and get something to drink." He took her hand and led her into the café, to one of the few unoccupied tables, one in the shadows in a corner.

They ordered, and not long thereafter, a waiter brought their sodas. Liddy sipped hers, then licked her lips. She looked up at Marek and shook her head. "I can't believe you even considered being one of those thugs—the Hitler Youth." She used a mildly derisive tone.

Marek looked puzzled at first. "Oh, that. I only said those things before to gauge where you and your family were politically." Marek studied his surroundings to make sure no one could hear them and lowered his voice to a whisper. "You know, I wasn't going to come right out and say I was a member of the underground resistance."

"You are?" Liddy gasped with surprise. "You mean a bona fide member?"

"Well, you don't have to officially join a group or anything. I just like to do what I can to help. I use my publishing experience to print pamphlets, leaflets, fliers—that kind of stuff."

"Oh, I see." She put the pieces all together as she recalled the time she had hidden at the window and Marek had pointed to some strange-looking equipment. "Somehow I just knew that. Well, I had a strong hunch, anyway," she said, then wished she could take it back.

"Really?" Marek said, a smile on his face.

"Where do you get the courage to do this?"

"I firmly believe that Hitler is doing some horrible things," he whispered. "If I ever have any doubts about my resolve, I search deep down, and God points the way." A moment of silence passed as Marek seemed to be in deep thought. He continued, "Besides, I have a great role model."

"Who's that?"

"Father Maximilian Kolbe, head of the Franciscan monastery where I worked. What an amazing man—I'll always remember him. He was such a humble servant of God. When the Germans invaded

Poland in the fall of '39 and took over the monastery, he ended up having to let most of us go.

"I'll never forget that day. Just think. With all the turmoil going on, he didn't know what would happen to his monastery. He had hundreds of workers. Or what about his newspaper with its thousands of readers? Instead, he focused on something he did know. He told us there were basically two enemies in the depth of every soul—good and evil, sin and love. So on that last day, his parting words surprised no one."

"What were they?"

"He said, 'Forget not love.' What a powerful moment. But wait. That's only half the story."

Chapter 14

"Tell me more," Liddy said. Even though terribly weary, she was determined not to miss the rest of the story.

"Father Kolbe was allowed to keep the monastery going," Marek said, "but they kept a close watch on him. When they discovered he had given refuge to hundreds of Jews, he was hauled away to the concentration camp at Auschwitz. Let me think—that was two summers ago, in '41. I just heard about one of the men who survived that camp. You won't believe his story."

Liddy's face perked up. "How did it end?"

"One of the prisoners escaped, so the others were then told that ten of them would be called out for special punishment. They'd be starved to death."

"How horrifying. I had no idea things were so bad in those camps."

"Father Kolbe would pray with others in the camp, and he befriended one inmate who was a father with young children. That man was chosen to be one of the ten. But Father Kolbe stepped forward and convinced the guard to take him instead. Right on the spot, he decided to give up his life for another. Can you believe that?"

Liddy shook her head in disbelief. "What an amazing sacrifice! How does a person come to do that, anyway?"

"It's hard to comprehend. Can there be any stronger evidence of faith in action?"

****

Herr Keppler sauntered into the bakery with his dog the next Thursday morning. But Keppler's typical flair was absent, as he struggled with a heavy bag draped over his right shoulder. Liddy had not seen him for several days.

"Here!" As he stood in front of the counter, he tossed the bag on a table near Liddy, who had busied herself scrubbing unoccupied tables. "I'm here to give you another chance. Use this, and maybe I'll become a regular customer again." A condescending sneer oozed out of his tight lips.

Mother came out of the kitchen, her suspicious stare glued to Keppler. "Good day, *Herr* Keppler," she said flatly.

Does Mother really want him back? "*Herr* Keppler has this bag for you, Mother."

Mother walked to the bag and looked inside. "Oh my, *Herr* Keppler! Where did you get all this?" She pulled out a bag of coffee and a small container of vanilla and motioned to Liddy to lift out the large bag of sugar.

"I have my sources," Keppler replied, a glint of pride in his eyes. "Now make those pastries the way they should be made. I paid dearly for these. I want free streusel cake for the rest of the month."

From the look on Mother's face, Liddy doubted whether her mother was in any mood to argue with the man. In seconds, Liddy's doubts were confirmed when Mother grabbed the bag and rushed back into the kitchen.

But Liddy, emboldened on this particular morning, decided to banter with Keppler a while. "How about we change the deal a bit, *Herr* Keppler? If you bring in two old shirts for my clothing drive at church, we'll add an extra week."

"What would you want my old shirts for?" Keppler replied. "Nobody would want those ragged old things."

"Someone who has just lost about everything in an air raid sure would. Don't you have a wife at home who could send us some freshly laundered shirts that you don't wear anymore?"

"No," came his curt answer. "She doesn't do my laundry anymore."

"Oh, is she limited in the way she can move like Mother? Is there something she needs prayer for?"

"No—she's gone, *Fräulein*. I've lived alone since she died. Besides, prayer would do no good. It didn't work for me."

"So sorry to hear about your wife. How long has it been?"

"A year. God really let me down—for the second time, I might add. First, my brother died … during the last war and then my wife. I've given up on God." He turned about-face and retreated with his streusel cake and coffee to a table.

Liddy stood quietly while she studied the man. Dare she follow him? She couldn't let the conversation end on that note. She grabbed the pot of coffee and edged toward him.

"*Fräulein*, I just sat down. I don't need a warm-up yet."

"*Herr* Keppler, you've suffered some terrible losses. I can understand how that heartbreak has challenged your faith."

"I'm doing fine, *Fräulein*. A strong person learns to get over it and move on."

"But you must know that not all prayers are answered the way we want, right? They are, indeed, listened to, and God has a plan. It may not align with your plan, though."

"Shows you how much we matter to God," he slurred.

"But you do matter," Liddy said. "God has suffered with you. He didn't just ignore your situation."

"*Fräulein,* enough of your preaching. There may have been a time when my faith was important to me, but once you've lost it, there's too much to overcome. I have a hard time believing any of that anymore."

"That's a shame. You're missing so much."

"Think about the resurrection, for one thing. It's so far-fetched. The Roman guards must have fallen asleep, and someone stole the body."

"Just a minute now, *Herr* Keppler. How does that explain the more than five hundred people who saw Christ on earth afterward? It wasn't only the apostles."

"Sure, sure. I wonder who did the counting."

"Paul talks about it in his first letter to the Corinthians."

"So? Anyone can write anything they want to make their case."

"But he wrote his letter at a time when most of those witnesses would have still been alive. Anyone could have asked a number of them to deny those claims."

"The more you look into it, *Fräulein,* the more you realize how different all the various accounts are. The Gospels don't agree on everything. They're imprecise. A lot of it must be made up." He took a large bite of his streusel cake and chewed with confidence.

"People don't see things the same way, *Herr* Keppler. Just imagine four of your most esteemed composers. Let's say they all witnessed the same wonderful event and were asked to describe it in the form of a new musical composition. None of the compositions would be alike; yet, they might all be masterpieces."

The tones of some not-so-masterful notes could be heard from the side room. Willy was limbering up for his morning practice. Keppler appeared anxious to move on. With Max at his side, he walked over to talk to him.

Liddy followed but watched from a distance.

"Have you perfected the national anthem yet?" Keppler growled at Willy.

Willy flinched at Keppler's direct question. "It's much better, sir." He hesitated for a moment. "Shall I play it for you?"

Liddy cringed. *Why would he subject himself to that exacting man?*

"Well, I've got a few more minutes," Keppler grunted.

Willy played the anthem through with few mistakes.

"That was very good," Liddy said from several paces away.

"You must continue to practice until you've got it down perfect," the officer said.

That comment from Keppler did not surprise Liddy, but what followed certainly did.

"What else have you been working on?" Keppler asked.

"My mother gave me the music for 'Ave Maria,' so I've been working hard to learn that."

Keppler sprang to full attention—it seemed he was now definitely in his element. "My, that's a challenging piece. I think of it as my favorite Franz piece—composed by Franz Schubert with piano arrangement by Franz Liszt." He stared for a moment at Willy but was met by a blank expression.

Really, Herr Keppler? Liddy thought. *Do you think he would know anything about composers?*

But then Keppler did something that Liddy never expected. "I'll play it for you. Get off the bench," he said with an authoritative motion of his arm.

Liddy's heart beat more rapidly ... with a new kind of fear. What kind of connection was being forged between these two: Keppler and her brother?

Willy got up from the bench and sat on the floor next to Max.

Keppler's fingers eased into the keys of the piano. The beautiful chords caused Max's ears to perk up. Willy slowly brought his hand to the dog's head and stroked with a gentle back and forth touch. Unlike before, this time, Max welcomed his attention as Willy continued to stroke the dog's head and back.

"Listen now," Keppler said. "Pay attention to the majestic pacing—so elegant yet so tender."

"Yes, *Herr* Keppler," Willy responded. He stared into Max's dark, glassy eyes.

The dog cocked his head to the side.

Liddy wondered whether her brother understood anything at all Keppler had said.

Keppler played on. "Now we soar with unsurpassed grace to the lofty notes and settle back in again. To me, it is breathtaking."

Keppler turned and faced Willy. The officer's eyes were now closed as if in a distant land, far away from any war. After a moment, he opened his eyes and exclaimed, "And that's how you're supposed to play it."

"How do you know so much about music anyway?" Willy asked.

"I used to be a music professor at the University of Berlin ... until the war came along and took priority," Keppler said.

Liddy raised her arms and muttered as she turned to leave, "A music professor? And with a musician's hands, no less." *I imagine he was a very strict teacher.*

"Who taught you how to play?" Willy asked. Curious, Liddy stayed to hear Keppler's answer.

"My older brother, Rolf. He was very talented, and he took me under his wing. That is, until World War I ended it all." Keppler's eyes turned glassy as he looked down. "He died because of that war—a war that disgraced Germany. Now we must show the world who we are." His jaw jutted forward with determination.

Willy sat motionless. "Tell me, *Herr* Keppler, who is your favorite composer?"

"Mendelsohn." Keppler paused then checked his watch. "Oh, no—I lost track of time. I'm running late. Come, Max. We must go."

"One more thing," Willy said. "I don't have the words to 'Ave Maria.' Do you?"

Keppler wagged his finger as he stood. "Forget about the words. You're not going to sing it, are you?" He looked off into the distance. "Oh, how my dear wife could sing it! She had one exquisite voice. I loved when she sang in the church choir." His mind appeared to drift to another time and then back again. "But, no, forget about the words. The music is the most important part. You concentrate on that—you must master that."

"But *Herr* Keppler—"

"What now?" Keppler glared back at him, anxious to leave.

"Isn't that like having streusel cake without the sugar?"

Liddy could see Keppler's patience wear thin. "Now, listen young man—"

"But you played it so special—even without the sugar."

The officer started to head into the main room when Willy called, "*Herr* Keppler?"

"Aren't you done *yet*, young man?"

"*Vielen Dank* (many thanks)."

Just then Marek, who had slipped out the front door, caught Keppler's attention.

"Who was that?" Keppler asked Liddy as she preceded him into the front room.

Liddy pretended not to hear and in an instant had popped into the kitchen.

She peeked through the small window to see Keppler in a rush out the door to catch up with Marek. *Oh no, he might follow Marek!* She looked out the front window. Marek had begun to ride his bike away but with little urgency. He struggled to maintain his grip on the handlebar with his one good hand. Meanwhile, Keppler bent over to retrieve something. It looked like Marek's handkerchief that he must have taken out to wipe down his bike. Keppler then motioned for Max to pick up Marek's scent.

Liddy knew at once what she needed to do. Marek was, no doubt, headed to the print shop, and she must warn him. She took off her apron and told her mother she'd be gone for a while. While she retrieved her bike, she figured a parallel route to reach Marek before Keppler. It was a route she had noticed on Marek's map, but it appeared to have far more traffic. This time, though, the traffic would have to wait for *her*.

Liddy started off and pedaled as fast as she could. *If only Marek could see me ride this fast,* she thought, her goose bumps larger the harder she pedaled. This time, stop signs did not deter her. She pulled out in front of slow-moving cars, ignoring the horns that blared away. She sped up and pressed on—even more determined. Jolts from the rough pavement rattled her every bone as the steady blur of buildings faded behind her.

As she pulled up to the print shop, Liddy was elated to see that Marek was safe as he was just entering the building. But then her heart sank. She would have to deal with Otto, the building's caretaker, who sat on the stoop.

As Liddy dropped her bike and approached Otto, he growled, "I remember you. What are you doing here again?"

"Otto, *mein Herr* … I don't have time to explain," Liddy said as she tried to catch her breath. "Marek is my friend … I'm on your side. A police officer will be coming around that corner any second now. Quick—I've got to hide Marek's bike. Please, I beg you, tell the officer that you saw a youth on a bike but he headed that way." She pointed in a different direction.

"Marek?" Otto said. "In trouble? Of course, I'll help."

Liddy wrestled with Marek's bike to get it to fit with her under the stairway. With an awkward grip on it, she had just gotten settled when she heard Keppler's voice.

"Heil, Hitler," he said. The words were not as strong as his typical salute as they came out between heavy breaths.

"Heil, Hitler," Otto responded.

"I'm in search of a young, dark-haired man on a blue bike. He went around the corner, and all of a sudden, he's disappeared. My dog is struggling with the scent. Did you see him?"

"I saw something out of the corner of my eye, Officer—headed west." He looked down at the tool in his hand and the toolbox beneath him on the next step of the stoop. "I've been busy sharpening my tools so didn't pay much attention."

"Can't be west," Keppler responded. "He'd still be in view."

Liddy's knees knocked together, and, despite the cold weather, her hands became moist with sweat. She lost her grip on Marek's bike. She lunged for it, just in time to keep the bike from crashing, but it still made a sound as it came to rest. She winced, gasped in fear, and peered out through a small crack in the stairway.

Otto's mind seemed ever so quick, as, in an instant, he dropped the tool he had sharpened into his box. It made a loud noise.

"What was that?" Keppler asked.

"What?" Otto responded as he appeared to pretend there was no earlier noise, but that it had come from the dropped tool he now looked at down in his box.

Liddy tried to focus on Keppler's face as her whole body shook.

Keppler gave Otto a look of distrust and turned to survey the surroundings. His eyes stopped on Liddy's bike. "Whose is that?" he asked.

"Oh, one of the tenants. She's Aryan, Officer. In fact, I can assure you, all of my tenants are Aryan."

With a clenched jaw, Keppler looked Otto straight in the eye as his hand clutched and then twisted the fabric of his shirt. "You better be telling me the truth, or you'll regret the day you lied to Conrad Keppler."

Chapter 15

"Women's clothing to the left, men's to the right," Liddy called out as several people filed down the stairs into the church basement Saturday afternoon. "You'll see bins marked for children and adults."

She picked up two bags of clothing that had been dropped off and began to sort through them, with shirts, pants, dresses, and shoes deposited into the nearby containers. Many of the items were in poor condition but would still be welcomed by those who now found themselves without.

Her head down in a bin of ladies' blouses, a familiar voice surprised Liddy. "Careful—be sure you're putting those items in the right place."

She looked up and exclaimed, "Marek, what are you doing here? I thought you had a commitment with *Frau* Solf."

"I did, but I remembered how disappointed you looked when I said I couldn't make it. I told *Frau* Solf that she would have to wait." He grinned as he shared the news. "I've made other arrangements."

"Well, I'm glad you have your priorities straight," Liddy said with a smile.

Marek nodded. "By the way, before I forget, *Frau* Solf asked if you could help a friend of hers. I told her you might be available for a few hours in the afternoon."

"For what?"

"I'm not sure. You should go talk to a *Frau* Elisabeth Von Thadden at the Red Cross office. She's anxious to meet you."

"I don't think so, Marek. I can't stand the sight of blood." Liddy wrinkled her nose and covered her mouth.

Marek chuckled. "I remember that expression. It's almost the same as what you gave me the last time I wore these." He pulled a couple of shirts from his rucksack. "Better that someone who really needs them gets these shirts."

"Great. I agree." She laughed. "How is your hand?"

"Not very good. You've probably noticed how it's slowed me down a lot in the bakery, especially with the *M* on the signature loaves. Maybe I should get you to do that part."

"I'll try, but only if you're patient and teach me."

"It's a deal."

Liddy stared at Marek in admiration. "Tell me, how did you know how to find my church?"

"I asked your mother. She was more than happy to share the address. And, by the way, she is very pleased that I can help you out."

****

A quiet afternoon in the bakery, Liddy took her time as she swept the floor. Although a chore she did not particularly like, it was still better than washing dishes—she knew a huge stack awaited her in the kitchen. However, she was glad to do both chores every day to save her mother from having to do them. Today while she worked, she smiled, content that Mother rested on the sofa while Father slept upstairs.

Her sweeping done, Liddy plodded into the kitchen to check out the stack that awaited her in the sink. But what a pleasant surprise! Willy on a stool, scrubbing diligently.

"Willy, what are you doing?"

"I wanted to do something nice for you before I leave for camp."

"How thoughtful of you. Looks like you're doing a great job."

"Well, do me a favor. Don't tell Mother I am this good at it."

"Hello, anybody here?" An unfamiliar female voice yelled from the front room.

Liddy hurried to check on the visitor.

A slender teenage girl had come in with a large manila envelope in her hand. A blue knitted cap topped her short, dark hair. "Is this where Marek works?"

"May I ask who are you?"

"My name is Anna. Marek wanted me to drop this off for him. He said he would pick it up in the morning."

"I'll make sure he gets it." Liddy took the envelope from the girl. As she did, she noticed an irregularity in the fabric of the girl's blouse, an outline of stitching in the shape of a star that had been removed. Anna, noticeably uncomfortable with Liddy's stare, turned to leave right away. "Thank you." She looked back while opening the door. She removed her cap to wipe her brow and straighten her hair.

Her profile looked familiar, and Liddy recognized her as the girl from the print shop. Uncertain what to say, she called out, "Great work Marek is doing," as Anna headed out the door.

"Yes, he's a very special fellow." Anna's words rang oh so true, yet still hurt as they continued to echo in Liddy's mind. Had they not come from another girl, they might have lingered softly with a sense of admiration; now they just rattled around and clamored harshly.

But not for long, as Liddy's attention shifted to the large envelope Anna had left behind, packed almost to the point of bursting. Did she dare take a peek inside? Marek wouldn't mind. Before she realized what she was doing, her fingers separated the loosely sealed flap.

****

Marek placed the large envelope into the basket of his bike. He wanted to deliver it to *Frau* Solf's place before dark and smiled when he saw that Anna had dropped it off the previous afternoon. *Frau* Solf had indicated that she expected a number of guests, and they would all be anxious to see the contents.

That evening, Marek rang the doorbell. Seconds later, as though she had been waiting for him, *Frau* Solf greeted Marek and invited him into the foyer, exactly the same as he remembered from earlier visits.

"Thank you for getting these to me on such short notice, Marek. How have you been?"

"Hectic times," he responded, then exhaled from deep within as if to give more emphasis to how he felt. "And then I managed to hurt my hand—that slowed me down." He handed over the envelope. "I hope you like these."

While *Frau* Solf opened the envelope, Marek cast a quick glance toward the living room and noticed that several guests had already arrived.

"These look terrific," said *Frau* Solf. "I'm going to show them off this evening. Did you also make up the false identification papers?"

"Yes. They're at the bottom of the stack."

"I see." She took a moment to look through them. "Excellent—much better than the ones you showed me before. By the way, I have another client for you. He's looking for a printer. Just a second—let me get his card." She retrieved her purse then rummaged through it. "Here it is. Keep this confidential," she said and handed over the card. Along with an address, it read:

Helmuth James Graf von Moltke

Once he had put the card into his pocket, Marek again looked into the living room and was taken aback. A figure that looked familiar sat in front of the wall of pictures that had haunted him earlier. Marek stepped aside so he wouldn't be seen and peeked around the corner to confirm his suspicions.

Dr. Reckzeh! Wouldn't Liddy be surprised to hear he was a member of the resistance? But would they dare tell Renate?

****

Several days later, *Frau* Von Thadden greeted Liddy at the downtown Berlin office of the Red Cross. The small office, even more crowded by surrounding bookcases, teemed with volumes small to very large.

"Thank you so much for meeting with me, Liddy. *Frau* Solf said you may be a great fit to help me out."

"I'm at a loss, *Frau* Von Thadden. I've never even met *Frau* Solf, and to be honest with you, I'm not too keen about doing anything at all medical."

"Well, as I understand it, a fellow named Marek really bragged about you—said you were very capable, extremely smart, and you had your priorities straight."

Liddy's smile widened with pride. "Oh, how nice of him, but what did you have in mind?"

She cleared her throat. "Let me find out a bit about you first. I heard you're working at your family's bakery. Do you enjoy that?"

"Well, I do what I must to keep it going, but I'm not exactly the best baker. I owe my time to my family, though—they really need me. I won't even be able to go on to college this year."

"But where is your heart? If we didn't have this horrible war, and you could do whatever you wanted, what would it be?"

"My dream has always been to become a history teacher."

"Outstanding! That's where my heart is as well. Before I got involved with the Red Cross, I used to run a boarding school for girls near Heidelberg. It was called the Evangelical School of Home Country Education for Young Women. My focus was to teach girls to become independent."

"That sounds wonderful. But why aren't you still there?"

"The Nazis made me shut it down due to 'activities endangering the state.'"

"What does that mean?"

"Oh, I was not very cooperative with the Nazis. I used to have some Jewish students, and we'd have worship services when we'd read some Psalms. The Nazis, of course, deemed them to be Jewish. Then, when I wouldn't hang a portrait of Hitler in the school, they nailed the doors shut."

"Sounds like you're not afraid to do things your way."

Frau Von Thadden shook her head. "No, it's that I want to do what I think is right in God's eyes. That brings me to why I asked you to meet with me. Do you have a couple hours free in the afternoons to tutor some children?"

"Tutor children?" Liddy gasped. "I thought you wanted me to apply bandages." She chuckled with a big grin.

"I understand you live in Pankow. I need someone on the northeast side to tutor eight children who struggled in school last year—ages nine to eleven. You can name the time you would be available."

"I'll have to check with my family."

"I can even pay you. I have some wealthy connections."

A surge of exhilaration charged through Liddy's veins. "It all sounds very exciting. I'd love to, but I have to think it through with my family. I'm not sure if they can do without me for a couple hours every afternoon. Maybe—I'll let you know."

"That's all I can ask. I can tell your heart's in the right place. Now it's just a matter of making it happen. Get back to me as soon as you can."

Chapter 16

E arly Wednesday morning, Liddy and Marek worked side by side in the kitchen.

"No, Liddy, not like that! Don't push the knife into the bread. You've got to cut back and forth."

"But it doesn't want to cooperate. It didn't come out of the oven right."

"Did you follow all my instructions for the dough?" His furrowed brow reinforced a condescending tone.

"I think so, but I'm not sure. Could I have forgotten a step?" She brought the palm of her hand to her forehead.

"Liddy, Liddy. You've got to follow each step precisely."

The clang from Liddy's knife hitting the table shattered the early morning serenity. She rubbed the back of her neck in frustration. Detail trimming of the letter *M* on the signature loaf didn't suit Liddy at all. She looked across the table at Marek. She felt vulnerable about her own baking abilities and decided it was time to turn the focus toward him. "Marek, I've got something to tell you. I know about your print room in that dilapidated building. I went there the other day to warn you because Keppler had followed close behind you."

"What? How did that come about?"

"He saw you leave here one day. You've got to be more careful—always leave out the back. Thank God, I beat him there. I had to work with Otto to get him off your trail, but that was too close a call. So, is that where you do all your underground printing?"

"Yes, Otto and the print shop have come in very handy. And he watches out for us—protects a bunch of underground people who live and work in that building. He feels there is no other choice but to defend human rights."

"Well, that rundown building must be a good cover for you all. I guess his caretaking is not so much for the building but more for you people."

"Yes, he's a terrific fellow."

With a steady hand, Liddy scraped a knife across the top of a measuring cup. Now that they had black-market ingredients from Keppler, they used the right amounts called for by the recipes—but not a granule more. "You said earlier you delivered some pamphlets to *Frau* Solf's house and saw Dr. Reckzeh there. Did you say hello?"

"No, I didn't know if he would like that I knew he was part of the underground. I kept my distance."

"And did *Frau* Solf like your pamphlets?"

"Like them? She thought they were downright terrific. She raved about the false papers. I must say I do have a knack for how to set up things for the best possible print job."

Marek began to braid long strips of rolled dough that now lay before him.

"The Solf Circle—they're quite the group of accomplished people, aren't they?" Liddy asked. "I was really impressed with *Frau* Von Thadden."

"Yes, they no doubt are people from the highest ranks of Berlin life—doctors, lawyers, diplomats, professors. How did your meeting with her go?"

"Oh, Marek—I'm excited!" Liddy's eyes were wide. "She wants me to tutor some children."

"Tutor?"

"Yes. I just don't know if Mother could handle my being gone."

"That *is* a problem, isn't it? Especially now that Willy won't be around."

"Yes, I'm going to talk to Father about it." She sprinkled cinnamon on the buns she had just made.

"With the Solf Circle," Marek said, "I've really got my foot in the door with an elite group. This could lead to some big things if this war ever ends."

"I'm happy for you, but I worry about how dangerous it is."

"Anything to do with the underground is dangerous, but it doesn't bother me. I owe it to my parents."

"I understand, and I want to support you. Your courage is a wonderful trait. But sometimes I shudder when I think of what might happen. I don't know if God has built me for this type of thing. Maybe I should put on blinders and focus on how to improve my baking or tutoring when I can."

"Go where you are feeling led." Marek paused a second. "Liddy, you're thinking too hard about it. Just follow your heart."

"But then I'm afraid there's no turning back."

"I know." His eyes looked distant.

"I'm sure glad I learned how to do print work," he continued. "Now I've got all these high-level contacts—all because I do a pretty good job."

"My, you're really showing your humility this morning!" Liddy smiled at her own sarcastic flair. "You're beginning to sound like what you told me your father is like."

Marek looked stunned. "Really?"

"I don't mean to hurt your feelings. I'm sorry. It's just that *Herr* Bonhoeffer said we all have inside of us a bit of something we are critical of in other people. I remember you talking about your father being such a boaster."

Marek thought for a moment. "Interesting—I guess this Bonhoeffer fellow must be right. Say, I know we delivered some letters for him, but I don't know much about him."

"Remember, he's a prisoner at Tegel prison where my father works. Pastor Bonhoeffer is being held for plotting to kill Hitler. Father says that in the last few years he's been active in promotion of what is called the Confessing Church."

"How is it different from the regular church?"

"Hitler has molded the German church to align with his narrow views. Jews are shut out of just about everything. Many leaders in the church have said nothing. But a bunch of people, including Bonhoeffer, have broken away. They say it's not right."

Marek nodded but then looked distracted. "Do you think I brag too much about my accomplishments?" he asked with eyebrows raised.

"No, not really. There's nothing wrong if we feel good about what we've done as long as we keep it in perspective. Sometimes we have to take the focus off of ourselves. *Herr* Bonhoeffer said we must remember what we owe to others. 'We receive more than we give,' he said. 'Life cannot be rich without such gratitude.'"

"Amen," Marek said. "I don't know where I would be without

Father Kolbe and the monastery." He continued to work on braiding some buns. "Of course, I can't forget the job my parents did raising me. They taught me so much. Lots of my recipes come from my mother—like these buns. My lessons started early too. I was in the kitchen helping her when I was only a six-year-old. I'll never forget that old mixer. It was always cutting in and out. Maybe that was her secret …" He swallowed hard and looked away.

"You really miss them, don't you?"

"I'll say. If only I knew where they are." His sigh brought a heavy exhale. "I have this terrible fear that they're suffering somewhere—not knowing is driving me crazy. I think about them and pray for them every day." Marek turned bright red with embarrassment as a steady stream of tears flowed down his cheeks. "I'm sorry."

"That's all right." Liddy got up, sidled next to Marek, and brought her head close to touch his. She gave him an understanding hug. "We need to keep praying for them—that's for sure."

When Mother came in unexpected, Marek was quick to turn away and wipe his face.

"Looks like you two are getting a lot done," she said with obvious sarcasm. "Liddy, I thought I told you last night to have extra dough ready for me to finish. Where is it?"

"Oh, Mother. That's right, you did. We've been talking here, and I completely forgot."

"I can't believe it, Liddy. Again? Where are your thoughts these days?"

By now, Marek had regained his composure, and he jumped right back into the conversation. "Actually, *Frau* Mittendorf, Liddy handed that responsibility to me first thing this morning. I'm the one who forgot. Blame me."

"Marek—" Liddy said, as fast as she could get his name out.

"Hush, Liddy. Let's get busy and get the work done." Mother turned about-face to leave. "I've got to get some aspirin for a headache. That's if Liddy has remembered to keep our stock replenished."

When her mother left, Liddy asked Marek, "Why did you take the blame for me?"

"It seems like you always get the blame. It was time for you to get a break."

****

The last meal together before Willy left for KLV camp in the country, dinner at the Mittendorf home that evening was a special affair. Mother had gone to great lengths to secure some schnitzel, Willy's favorite. With the food served, everyone sat, then bowed their heads. Father's prayer had a special focus—God's protective care of Willy.

"Thank you, Father," Willy said. "I'm not happy about going, but I am still kind of excited about seeing the Anhalter Train Station tomorrow."

"Well, it's the adventure of it all. But no doubt, we're going to miss you."

"I'll say we'll miss you," Mother said. Her eyes glistened.

The reality of Willy's leaving began to sink in for Liddy as well. "You'll really get to escape all the suffering and drudgery of this awful war."

"For sure," Mother added. "Without a doubt, it's wearing me down. I wish we could all go with you." A brief glimmer of false hope flashed across her eyes.

"I think what we all need is a good dose of spiritual encouragement," Father said. "Maybe now, before Willy leaves, I should relay some things from prisoner Bonhoeffer."

Mother perked up and smiled at Father.

"Bonhoeffer talked about the Stations on the Road to Freedom. There are four steps: Discipline, Action, Suffering, and Freedom. By freedom, he means an eternal home with a loving God in heaven. But the starting point is discipline."

"Oh, no," Liddy exclaimed. "I'm not off to a good start. I'm terrible at self-discipline. I'm too scatter-brained."

"He said that we start with mastery over sense and soul," Father said. "We learn the secret of freedom only through control—"

"*Herr* Keppler," Liddy interjected. "Now *there* is someone who has control. He is disciplined."

"He appears to be on the outside," Father said. "But to what? I think it all begins with obedience—being totally obedient to the word of God. Then once you've mastered that, you can focus on action. We need to dare to do what is right through deeds and service—not just thoughts."

"I think most people want to do the right thing in their minds," Mother said, "but when it comes to doing it in reality, that's another story."

"In particular if there's some risk involved," Liddy added.

"Well, Bonhoeffer goes on to say that if we encounter danger, rather than react in fear, we should direct our energy to the redeeming love of Christ for all who suffer. Suffering is to be expected just as Christ suffered. Then, in the end, when we die, we reach eternal freedom, our ultimate goal."

"He seems like a very wise man, Klaus," Mother said. "I like the way he divides it into steps, or as he says, stations. I think most of us are at different points along the way to freedom." She looked over at Willy's half-full plate of food. "Young man, this is your special meal. I don't want to find even the slightest morsel left on that plate."

"Don't worry, Mother." Willy took another bite with a pensive look on his face. "But, Father, I'm not sure I understand any of this. So where am I in these steps?"

"Well, you've accepted Christ, and you're trying to be obedient to His word. You've done a bit of the others, but you have a whole lifetime ahead of you. A good start for you now is to be brave while you're away at camp."

"So does the discipline part lead to courage?" Liddy asked. "It's the courage part that intrigues me. I have a wonderful story of courage to tell you all that I heard from Marek. Do you want to hear it?" She did not wait for a response and instead started right in. "It's about Father Kolbe, the founder and head priest at the City of Mary Monastery. A couple of years ago, in a prison camp, he volunteered his life in exchange for another man who was a father of children." Liddy went on to describe all the details as Marek had relayed them to her. When done with the story, she asked, "Would you do that? How does a person get the courage to give up his life for another?"

"I think I know," Father said. "Our pastor talked about it in a sermon a while back." He got up to retrieve the family Bible. He thumbed through to find the appropriate passages. "Here it is, Luke 12:11–12: 'Do not be anxious … for the Holy Spirit will teach you in that very hour what you ought to say.' Then the next step is to actually act upon that. In Jeremiah 7:23, the Lord said, 'Obey my voice, and I will be your God, and you shall be my people. And walk in all the ways that I command you, that it may be well with you.'"

Chapter 17

"Have you ever seen so many people in one place, Willy?" Klaus asked as he tried to talk above the noise of the crowd that had gathered early that morning at the Anhalter Train Station.

"How much longer do we have to wait, Father?"

Klaus looked at his son and then at the large clock on the far wall of the station. "It's going to be about fifteen minutes. That's when we're supposed to meet a *Frau* Schmidt with our bags by the loading area."

"Why couldn't Mother and Liddy come down with us?"

"This trek would have worn out your mother. As for Liddy, someone had to stay home to help watch the shop—especially in the morning. Besides, you got to say your good-byes to them earlier. You know they love you very much."

Busyness crowded the station as many people walked to and fro—some looked to see the time on their watches, others struggled to make headway under the weight of their heavy bags.

Willy's knees twitched, and his lips quivered. Klaus began to lament his son's anxiety. Then when Willy looked up at him and asked, "Do I have to go?" he, too, felt uneasy.

Klaus lowered his head. "I can barely hear you over the noise." He noticed Willy's moist eyes and put his arm around him and leaned closer. "Yes, son. I'm sorry, but cheer up. Once you get there, you'll soon feel right at home."

"I hope so." Willy glanced around the station. Klaus detected a brief smile when he recognized someone. "Oh, good. There's my friend Rudy. I almost forgot he was going to my camp too. Maybe this won't be so bad after all. But I'm going to miss my piano," he said, his voice soft and a look of resignation on his face.

"I know," Klaus said. "But you'll be able to play again when you come home. It will still be waiting for you—I promise. Don't worry."

"*Herr* Keppler showed me how to play 'Ave Maria.' He's really good. I like it when he plays the piano."

"I heard about that episode from your sister."

"Did you know that since then he's sat down with me a couple of times? He doesn't get so mad anymore when I make mistakes."

"Really? I hadn't heard that," Klaus responded with surprise.

"He actually shows me how the fingers are supposed to move. Mother can't really show me, so it doesn't always sink in. And you know what? I even like *Herr* Keppler's dog now. We've made friends." Willy gazed out at the bustling crowd, then reflected, "Why do you suppose *Herr* Keppler is so cross with people all of the time?"

"You know, Willy, part of it is just his personality; part of it is the stress of the war. It's a terribly tough time for all of us. From what I've heard from Liddy, I think he struggles to figure out which he loves more—his music or his country. It's a shame, but God is far down on his list at this particular time."

"*Herr* Keppler's really scary, but he's not an evil person, is he?"

"We can object to the bad things he does or the evil that has taken over his heart, but it's not our place to judge him as a person. The Bible teaches us not to judge. *Herr* Bonhoeffer says that judging others makes us blind. He says that by judging, we blind ourselves to our own evil and to the grace that others are as entitled to as much as we are. Love, on the other hand, is illuminating."

Willy scratched his head, and with a puzzled look, he mouthed, "Il-lum-in-a-ting. So you're saying he's not all bad, right?"

"Of course not. He's a child of God too." Klaus bent over again and grasped his son's chin; a gentle nudge brought it upward. "Willy, you're only eight years old—you're not expected to understand everything. This is a very complicated world. The only thing we know for sure is that God will be there for us."

Klaus looked up at the clock. "Well, let's go, son. It's time to gather the bags and get them to the loading area."

A train whistle blared in the distance. It wasn't the first whistle they had heard that day, but it lingered the longest.

"Think of it as starting a new journey, son," Klaus said, now with a quiver in his own voice. "I guess that whistle marks the end of one, the beginning of the next."

****

With Mother busy in the kitchen, Liddy approached her parents' bedroom door, which was ajar. From the room, she could hear the radio announcer say, "The Allies are approaching Rome …" She tapped a soft knock on the door, but since she knew her father would soon leave for work, she didn't wait for a reply before she walked in. Sitting at his desk with an envelope in his hand, and caught off guard, he fumbled to insert a letter.

Liddy raised her eyebrows. "What is that? Wait—I recognize that writing. Isn't it another letter from Pastor Bonhoeffer? What are you doing with it open?"

Without a response, Father sealed the envelope.

"Father, don't tell me you've been opening his letters and reading them!"

"It's not as bad as it looks, *meine Liebchen*. All of his letters get read by someone at the prison. He's a political prisoner. I'm just one more reader."

"But, Father, that doesn't make it right. Isn't it still someone's personal information that you're not authorized to see? I can't believe you would do such a thing."

"I know, I know. Forgive me. But haven't you ever been tempted to look at something you shouldn't have?"

Guilt flooded Liddy's soul as she recalled her episode with Marek's envelope. "I guess I have," she replied sheepishly. "It's so easy to rationalize it. I did it with something of Marek's because I thought he wouldn't mind. But that doesn't make it right."

Again, Father had no response.

"I see—now I'm putting it all together," Liddy said. "Does that explain all the words of spiritual wisdom you've shared with us lately at the dinner table?"

"Yes," he responded with a deep sigh. "I've so wanted to impress your mother. I guess I got carried away. I meant no harm." Father looked at the envelope and paused. "I'll have to confess to *Herr*

Bonhoeffer—that would be the right thing to do."

"That makes sense. Maybe we're all so affected by the stress of this war, we do things we wouldn't normally do."

"Ah, yes … stress. I haven't wanted to tell your mother, and please don't tell her yourself." He opened the drawer on the right side of his desk. "See the stack of bills in here? I don't know how we're going to pay them all this month. The dry goods store called and has cut off our credit."

"Things are that bad?"

"People aren't coming in as much. Even sales of the *M* signature loaves are way down."

Liddy looked down, this time, a flood of embarrassment coursing through her veins. "Probably because I'm not making them as well as Marek."

"No, no—I don't think it's that."

"I came in here to ask you something, but now I'm not sure I should."

"What? Tell me. Please."

"*Frau* Von Thadden wants me to tutor some children for a few hours in the afternoons. Do you suppose Mother would be able to handle things on her own?"

Father shifted in his chair. He scratched his head and tilted it from side to side, but did not respond right away. "Well, I don't know," he finally said, then pursed his lips and glanced out the window. "We could ask her, but would she be straight with us?"

"I can tell you're not too keen about it, Father." Liddy's shoulders slumped. "Forget about it." She turned to leave. The well-being of the bakery must come first—there was no question about that. She stopped at the door, turned to her father, and tried to smile, but only

sighed. "As I think again about *Herr* Bonhoeffer, don't you agree
he would want to share his thoughts with you anyway? Why be so
sneaky? You know, maybe he'll even take you under his wing out of
sympathy." She forced a chuckle.

"Liddy, there's a whole new dimension he's brought to my
thinking. He's challenged it several times, but you wouldn't believe
how hard my mind works to bury it and not face up to it. With
this wretched war, I've often sought comfort from the Twenty-
third Psalm. You know, 'Yea though I walk through the valley of
the shadow of death, I will fear no evil, for Thou art with me.' And
I know that to be true without question. But *Herr* Bonhoeffer goes
even further—we can't be content to just not fear evil. He said that
'silence in the face of evil is evil itself.' I've been so focused on the
survival of the bakery that I've missed the big picture."

Liddy stood in quiet awe. "I would say we all have, Father."

****

Thursday morning brought a surprise visit from someone quite
familiar to Mother.

"Dr. Reckzeh, it's so good to see you again. What brings you in
so early?" she asked as Liddy stood nearby.

"I'm meeting someone here," he said. "I'll get my pastry and
coffee and sit at a table. How have you been? You're looking well."

"I'm surviving," Mother replied. "But one of these nights all the
frantic response to an air raid might do me in."

Liddy relished the fact that her mother was becoming more
adept at everyday pleasantries. Maybe she tried harder because of
Dr. Reckzeh's handsome looks. Liddy chuckled to herself.

A few minutes later, *Herr* Keppler arrived. Ever since he provided the Mittendorfs with sugar and once in a while coffee from the black market, he had become a regular again.

Keppler ordered his streusel cake and took it with his coffee to the back of the room. Liddy watched every move he made, and when he set his items next to Dr. Reckzeh and the men shook hands, she slipped into the kitchen to tell Marek, who had just finished his work for the day.

"What!" Marek exclaimed. "It can't be!" They had not yet told Mother about the doctor being a part of the underground. What was he doing with Keppler?

Marek peeked through the window of the kitchen door and watched as Dr. Reckzeh pointed to a piece of paper. Keppler had a rare smile on his face.

"Liddy, we need to find out what they are talking about. It looks like the doctor has some sort of list. Go out and pour some coffee. Hurry."

"You really want me to go out there and snoop around those two?"

"Don't worry. They both know you. They won't be suspecting a thing."

"Besides, what's left of that pot of coffee must be like tar." Liddy tried to talk her way out of going. "They won't be too happy with that."

"That's your imagination. You just served them from that pot. We must act now! You can do it, Liddy, I know you can. Hurry."

Liddy retrieved the coffee pot, and with cautious steps approached the table. In between pours, she glanced at the list. She took a moment to get a better look, but *Herr* Keppler must have sensed her closeness, as he drew the paper to his chest and growled, "*Fräulein*! You aren't snooping into things that are none of your business, are you?"

"Oh no, *mein Herr*." Liddy backed away and hurried to the kitchen.

"You're right, Marek. It's a list of people's na-names." Liddy spoke so fast she tripped over her words.

"Think—do you remember any of them?" Marek's concerned eyes widened as he rubbed his forehead.

"Well, the first one at the top of the list was really short. It started with an 'S.' Marek, I'm afraid it was *Frau* Solf's name!"

"I can't believe it! Why that dirty, rotten …" Marek pounded his fist on the table. "I've got to warn *Frau* Solf. Her whole circle is in danger."

"Oh, no!" Liddy said. "That would mean *Frau* Von Thadden too."

Startled by Marek's outburst, Mother joined them from the far end of the kitchen. "What's this all about?"

"Liddy, explain it to your mother. I've got to get going. I'll go out the back door. Wait. I just thought of something. *Herr* Moltke is probably in danger too. He has to be warned. I can't get to both places today, but—"

"I'll go," Liddy said.

"Go where?" Mother probed. "What's going on?"

"You would really go on your own?" Marek asked. "Let me see where it is." He pulled out the card that Frau *Solf* had given him. "It's on Derfflinges Strasse right near Tiergarten Park, where we had the picnic. Do you remember how to get there?"

"Where are you going, Liddy? And why?" Mother's anger and confusion raised her voice to a high pitch.

"You can count on me," Liddy said to Marek.

He shot her a quick smile and rushed out the back door.

"Liddy, please tell me what's going on!" Mother demanded.

Liddy gave a hurried explanation while Mother listened with wide eyes. "I don't understand," she said. "Dr. Reckzeh seems like such a nice man. I can't be too upset with him if he just wants to support his country and his government. This country has been so downtrodden since World War I. A lot of people want to see Germany rise again as a powerful nation."

"Yes, like Keppler," Liddy said. "Blind service to your country. Don't you understand, Mother? At some point, you have to stand up and confront evil. God must come before country!"

Mother thought for a moment. "God before country. I like the sound of that. To think how much I admired Dr. Reckzeh at first. Now I realize that maybe he's not the person I thought he was." She caught her breath and wiped her brow. "Right now this is all too complicated for me."

"Well, I don't have time to talk about it anymore," Liddy said. "I've got to head out to Tiergarten."

"Liddy—please be careful. I worry so much about you."

"Mother, do you think I want to make you worry on purpose? I'll be fine."

****

"And who might you be?" A lady of medium build in her early thirties with short dark hair and round facial features answered the door. Her makeup and finely tailored navy-blue dress portrayed "upper class."

"My name is Liddy Mittendorf. *Frau* Solf sent me."

"Ah, yes. *Frau* Solf. Please step in."

"Is *Herr* Moltke here?" Liddy asked.

"No, I'm sorry. He's tending to some matters. I'm Freya von Moltke. May I help you?"

"I have some important news for you."

"Please come in." *Frau* Moltke led her to into a large living room with fine furnishings. "Please have a seat."

"I may as well be straightforward about all this. *Frau* Solf, herself, didn't send me, but I am quite familiar with her organization. My friend Marek has told me all about it."

Frau Moltke leaned back and looked at Liddy askance. "So how is it you know *Frau* Solf, and who is this Marek? Is he a member of the Solf Circle?"

"No, but he provides them with printed leaflets, and *Frau* Solf had directed him to offer to do the same for your group. We fully support any resistance efforts against Hitler, and that's why I'm here—to give you a warning. You may be in danger."

Frau Moltke again looked at Liddy with apprehension. "Well, this is a very dangerous world. Aren't we all distrusting of others?"

"Let me get straight to the point," Liddy said. "Do you know a Dr. Paul Reckzeh?"

Frau Moltke thought for a moment. "No, I can't say that I do."

"It appears that Dr. Reckzeh has been infiltrating underground organizations. My friend Marek saw him at a Solf Circle meeting earlier. Just this morning, I personally saw him hand over a list of names to the authorities. *Frau* Solf's name was on that list."

Frau Moltke's head jerked back. "That could prove disastrous. I'll have to contact my husband right away—he's at our summer farmhouse up in Kreisau. I know he had already identified one possible informant and reported his name to *Frau* Solf. I don't know if this is the same one." She shook her head and reached down with a trembling hand to smooth her dress.

Liddy waited … and stared at the woman in deep thought.

"My first priority is to reach my husband," *Frau* Moltke said. She paused again. "What is a person supposed to do these days? We are only trying to do the right thing—for Germany and all of mankind. We're totally against this war. And we don't care about Hitler. If he gets killed, though, we're afraid he might become a martyr. It's all so sickening. And my husband's entire family has a proud tradition of accomplishment for this country. His great-grand-uncle was a key general in the Prussian War. And now we have all this." She shook her head again.

Liddy sat in silence and stared into the distance. She marveled at the woman's story. She realized they were kindred spirits caught up in a horrible war, and there was indeed no turning back.

Frau Moltke continued, "My husband has always told me he's not a Protestant, not a great landowner, not an aristocrat, not a Prussian, not a German, but a Christian and nothing else."

Those words seemed to say it all. Liddy expressed that she must be off, and departed in haste.

Chapter 18

July 26, 1944 (About one year later)

Meine liebste Grossmutter,

It's been such a long time since I've written you—I'm so sorry for that! I know Mother has a hard time writing, so it's really up to me. I wish I were more disciplined about it. My leaving so abruptly last summer still leaves a sour taste in my mouth. You'll be pleased to hear that the fire didn't totally set me back with my historical pictures. I found many of the negatives right here at home!

I hope and pray that all is well with you and Grossvater! We in Berlin are all managing to get by in spite of this horrible war. Keeping the bakery going has been a real struggle. We wish we would get more customers, but I don't want you to worry about that.

Willy has finally gotten used to being at school at KLV camp. After a year, it's about time. As you know, he didn't want to go, but he's made some new friends. Mother's heart has ached for him all this time. We wish he would write more often, but I guess that's a lot to ask of a nine-year-old. Last time we heard from him, he mentioned he might be getting a piano—probably one that's been confiscated. At any rate, it's very exciting, as he's missed playing so much.

Willy also said he's not able to get much sleep because there are railroad tracks nearby. Early one morning he happened to see a train go by with the cars so packed, some people almost fell off. He wasn't sure where it was heading.

We are all very busy. Unfortunately, Mother's physical condition has gotten steadily worse, with lots of pain all day long. I have been more tuned into that and have tried to pick up more of the load. We've learned to deal better with the air raids now too. Mother has worked out a new routine for getting into the cellar. She sits and moves down each step on her bottom. It takes a while but she's always made it. So far, I'm happy to report there have been no slivers either! By the way, I always think of you when we're stuck down in that cellar. It's times like that when you think of the ones you love the most.

I'm really enjoying learning to knit with the yarn and needles you sent me for Christmas. Thank you again. I just wish I had more time for it!

Last time I wrote, I mentioned Marek, who works here early mornings. We are getting to know each other well—he's a special young man. He has pushed me to come out of my shell, and we've had some great times exploring Berlin. With a printing background, he's also helping me to compile my pictures into a book. Unfortunately, he remains saddened by the disappearance of his parents and anxiously awaits some news. We all pray that God will deliver them.

Father enjoys his nighttime job at the prison because he has befriended a pastor there. Herr Bonhoeffer has offered to spend time with him to share his spiritual wisdom. Father then passes it on to the family to the delight of us all.

This war sure has dragged on. Do you wonder about the future of Germany? Marek has heard about some underground groups where all the members have been arrested—over seventy of them! With the Normandy invasion in June, who knows what will happen?

I've saved the best for last. Mother received word that Willy will be allowed to make a trip back home for a weekend visit before the start of the next school year. He'll come via bus the evening of August 18. Mother has marked it on her calendar and is counting off each and every day. I promise I'll write you afterward to let you know how he is doing. I know he won't write. He'll be too busy, I'm sure.

Enough for now. Stay safe. May God bless you, Grossmutter, and pass my love on to Grossvater! You are both always in my thoughts and prayers.

Viel Liebe,
Liddy

Chapter 19

When Liddy shared with him that she had corresponded with her grandmother, Marek became jealous. He so looked forward to receiving a letter from one of his parents, or even any sort of communication from someone who knew about them.

One day, several months earlier, a letter from Micah, his best friend, arrived. He had disappeared on the same day over a year ago. Marek was so happy to hear from him but disappointed he knew nothing of his parents' whereabouts. Micah had written from the Dachau concentration camp. At length, he described the deplorable conditions there.

Marek did not like to reread the letter often, but late some evenings he found himself obsessing over it. Slumped in a side chair, he would read the scribbled words by a dim light, sometimes falling asleep deeply troubled, his hand still clutching the letter.

****

Horrid conditions existed that day at the Ravensbrück concentration camp, ninety kilometers north of Berlin. Two train cars of women had arrived from different locations at the same time, one from Auschwitz, Poland. Guards shouted instructions for the women to form two lines: one for the elderly or those who had children with them, another for all others.

A lady, a bit taller than those around her, seemed to know the routine as if she had been through this sorting process before. Although her head was turned back toward those behind her, she stood straight and looked strong and able-bodied. It was evident that those who appeared physically capable had value because they would be good workers; others were no doubt considered expendable.

Some of those in line stood out—they carried a few prized possessions stuffed into suitcases and bags of all shapes and sizes. Little did they know they soon would be stripped of all their worldly belongings, including their clothes. Their bodies would be shaved, and they would be issued standard wear with wide vertical stripes.

Stoic resignation seemed to shroud the mood of every prisoner, and they all stood in abject silence. After dozens of others passed through, the tall lady arrived at the front of her line.

"Name?" the clerk asked.

"Sophie Menkowicz."

"Place of birth?"

"Warsaw, Poland."

"Arriving from?"

"Auschwitz."

"Jewish?"

"Yes."

"Children with you?"

"None." Maybe that prompted her to think of her son, Marek, as a guard barked commands to keep moving, and she was pushed along to the next checkpoint. She received a small, dirty food bowl and a smock with a yellow triangle on it.

What would Marek look like now? she might wonder, shutting out the shouts of the guards to keep moving. *Has he grown into a strapping young man? Is he safe?* She undoubtedly wanted to believe so. It had been more than a year—too long ago. Yet, somehow, could it be possible, she might feel closer to him at this moment?

Sophie and the other women arrived at their new living quarters—but the word "living" seemed out of place. Maybe it should have been called "survival quarters." Hundreds of women were jammed into each barrack. Six of them would have to share a small wooden platform with no mattresses that served as a bed.

An older lady stood next to Sophie, shaking her head. "I can't believe that six of us will fit into that space."

"I've done it before," Sophie responded as she tried to encourage the others. "Trust me, you get to know each other sooner than you can imagine." She extended her hand. "I'm Sophie from Poland," she said in German.

"And I'm Betsie from Holland."

****

The guards herded all of the women out to perform a full day of hard labor in the trenches. They were pushed along in a line, one behind the other. Sophie kept checking on Betsie.

"It's important to stay on your feet and keep moving," Sophie whispered to her. They arrived at the trenches, and each woman grabbed a pickaxe or a shovel as they began their day of hard work.

As Sophie dug, how could she not wonder about much better times with a shovel—times with her son, Marek? When he was about ten, the entire family had spent an afternoon planting a pine tree. It had been a damp day, and she had always said the covering of mud on Marek's body was direct evidence of how hard he had worked. She no doubt wished she could see that tree now, and imagined how Marek would look at it fondly and admire how tall it had grown.

A groan of fatigue from Betsie prompted Sophie to look back toward her. She was wiping her brow.

"The secret is to pace yourself," Sophie said. "But never look like you're slacking off or the guards will harass you. You want them to like you. If they do, you might get a favor or two. I've heard there's a shoe repair shop here. That wouldn't be a bad place to work."

When Betsie stopped for a moment, Sophie added, "Better keep your head to your work."

"I'm trying to find my sister," Betsie whispered. "I know she is here, but I lost track of her ever since we arrived."

****

A stream of dark smoke wafted up from the tall chimney of the crematorium—a stark reminder of the fate of the less fortunate. The camp had many rows of barracks—long structures with low-sloped, gabled roofs and small square windows. Each housed hundreds of women. Part of the camp was enclosed with walls made of aggregate, other parts by barbed wire fences. A tall watchtower allowed guards to survey the surroundings, aided by lamps hanging from high posts.

The prisoners gathered for their evening meal—the only one they would get for the day. It was a bowl of broth and a piece of dry bread. "Is there anything in here?" Betsie asked as she swirled her spoon through the brown liquid in her bowl, in hopes she'd stir up a bite or two.

"If you're lucky, you might find a pea or something you probably wouldn't even recognize, anyway. That's if you're lucky," Sophie repeated. "Or if you get to know the server."

At the end of the day, after many hours of hard work, they gathered in the barracks, and Betsie offered to lead anyone who wanted to pray. Sophie and several others listened. After the prayer, Sophie pulled Betsie aside.

"So you're a Christian," Sophie commented to Betsie. "I know I'm here because I'm Jewish. But what's someone like you doing here?"

"My whole family got into trouble because we harbored Jews," Betsie said. "My father always taught us that Jews are God's chosen people. He thought what the Nazis were doing was horrible. In fact, he actually built a hiding place for several people." She paused. "One day the Nazis got wind of it all, though."

"And you ended up at this wretched place."

"Yes, my entire family got rounded up that day, but I'm not sure how many are here."

"Round-up day for us included my husband, me, and a family friend," Sophie said. "Sometimes I wish my son had been there just so we would all be together. But I know that's foolish thinking. Besides, we're all separated now anyway; I have no idea where my husband is. I pray that he and my Marek are safe. That's what keeps me going—I think about them and the day that we might all be back together."

Marek stirred and awoke from his dream, his fingers still grasping the letter.

****

"*Herr* Bonhoeffer, what are you doing in the infirmary so late at night?" Klaus asked soon after he had reported to work for his night shift at the Tegel prison.

"One of the other guards brought me down. A patient with high anxiety had been calling out for God. I came down to pray with him."

"Believe me. I know many of them value that and look forward to seeing you."

"It's a special time for me to be able to share God's love."

Klaus nodded, then asked, "What news do you have about your trial?"

"They keep putting it off. I've been at this place for over a year and still have no idea what lies ahead for me. The only thing I am certain of is a future home with my Savior."

"The days must be terribly long. It's good that they at last have let you go outside to the exercise area."

"Yes, I relish that. It's a welcome break. A seven-by-ten cell with a plank bed can be very depressing. I also get the latest war news from some of the hired help here in the infirmary." He drew closer to Klaus and lowered his voice. "Is it true things are moving in the right direction?"

Klaus responded with a slight nod.

"Did you hear that they allowed a visit by my betrothed, Maria? Much to my dismay, though, with a room packed full of visitors, it was superficial. "I wanted to express to her how I truly felt, but I've only been able to write it in a letter. I'm not embarrassed to tell you the truth. I told Maria in the letter how I looked forward to our tender embrace, how I longed to stroke the sorrow from her brow." Bonhoeffer sighed deeply. "I was thrilled to, at least, see her in person. I thank the dear Lord for that."

Klaus nodded again.

"She brought me this book." He pulled the book from inside his shirt and showed Klaus. "I've known you for some time now, Mittendorf, and I feel comfortable letting you in on a little secret." His eyes discreet, he surveyed his surroundings. "We've been marking certain letters on different pages very lightly as a form of code. That's the only way we've been able to communicate in secret."

"Well, as we both know, your letters have been read by many people," Klaus said. "I've confessed to my role in that."

"Yes, but this shouldn't have to continue much longer. I think it's only a matter of time before the Third Reich falls. I hope I can ride it out until then."

Klaus leaned closer. "Quite a number of people from the underground hope that as well. Think of all those members of the Solf and Kreisau circles arrested last January. Their time may be up."

"Yes, indeed. It's a shame. The war would probably be over by now if there had been more people like them. So many have been content to sit back and accept evil."

"You've shown great courage through your suffering," Klaus said. "Haven't you also said a person doesn't have to shout from the rooftops, but maybe try to be effective from within?"

"Yes. I've worked through my sermons, my teachings, the Confessing Church, and even behind the scenes with the *Abwehr*."

"The central intelligence organization?"

"Yes." The pastor paused for a moment, then continued: "What people needed to do was to get on the right train to begin with. If you board the wrong train, it's no use running along the corridor in the other direction."

"You're right," Klaus replied. "Too many jumped on the wrong train or just stood by, willing to look the other way."

"Mittendorf, you have been a good friend, and we have prayed together many times, but I must remind you that confession of guilt happens without a sidelong glance at the others, who are also guilty."

"I'm not sure I understand."

"I think true confession is when you look only at yourself. Don't try to soften your feelings by thinking of others' guilt."

Klaus half smiled.

Chapter 20

err Keppler wouldn't admit it to anyone, but in reality, he looked forward to his time with Willy at the piano. Maybe, at last, he came to see in Willy a bit of himself, the young protégé of an accomplished mentor. Keppler's mentor had been his older brother, Rolf, who had exceptional talent. Truth be told, Keppler had been jealous of that talent. Oh, how he wished he could play like his brother. Rolf played well enough that even as a young man he was asked to be the organist at their weekly Mass. Keppler would never forget the look of pride on his mother's face the first time that happened.

More than just a piano teacher, his brother had taught him almost everything he knew, from how to ride a bike, to playing ball, to solving a tough problem at school, to table manners. It was Rolf who had insisted on the use of a metronome so he would improve his timing while he played the piano. To this day, Keppler blamed that nasty device for his obsession with being on time.

Rolf was also the one who had guided him in his love for his homeland. He knew by heart every patriotic song in the book. In fact, "*Das Deutschlandlied*" became his theme song. They also spent hours talking about past heroes in German history, and when Rolf left to become one of those heroes during the Great War, Keppler's pride overshadowed his sadness.

But then tragedy struck. Rolf incurred significant injuries and spent a long time recovering at a convalescent home. Eventually, to the family's delight, Rolf came home, where Conrad Keppler played soothing piano for him hour after hour. However, Rolf never made a full recovery and passed away. And Conrad?

He obsessed about the loss of his brother and best friend. He often found himself in reverie as he recited a simple poem that honored the brother whom he loved so much:

A true brother he was; I loved him dearly.
Taught me all I know—can't express it more clearly.
Talent he had; he could master any tune,
How can I trust God, when He took him so soon?

* * * *

"It's been quite a while since I've heard anything out of that piano," Keppler said as he approached *Frau* Mittendorf on Monday morning. "When does your son come home from KLV camp?"

"I'm counting the days—only five more. Do you want your usual?"

He nodded, and after he received his morning staple, he headed to "his" table.

Liddy, who stood in the shadows of the kitchen, watched Keppler's every move, then followed him to his table. "*Herr* Keppler, you seem to have a connection to that piano. If you don't mind if I ask, I'd like to know why."

"I have no idea what you mean, *Fräulein*."

"You seem so intent on hearing Willy play, and he hasn't even been around for months. But I bet when he finally does show, you'll do nothing but criticize him. I don't understand why he'd even risk it. If I were him, I wouldn't be in any hurry to get home to play for you."

"And what's it to you anyway? I expect perfection from him because that's what was expected of me."

"Who did that? Your parents?"

"No, my brother. The one God abandoned."

Liddy remained quiet a moment as those words sank in. "It sounds like you've given up on God. Tell me then, where does your heart truly lie?"

"It's none of your business, but be assured, I have my priorities in life sorted out. Are you done snooping?" The tone of his voice left no doubt of his irritation.

"But if I may, *Herr* Keppler, I'd like to say something more."

Keppler sipped his drink and said nothing.

"Imagine you are at Schiller Hall downtown, and a huge audience is clapping for you. The applause is deafening."

Keppler released the slightest hint of a smile, his eyes … his thoughts … drifted to some distant imaginary crowd.

Liddy continued, "Tell me, is the applause because you've just done a terrific job playing your favorite composition, or is it because you've just received an award of merit for contributions to a great war victory?"

Keppler sat in silence. Finally, he asked, "How about you, *Fräulein*? Would you be receiving an award for the best streusel cake?" He chuckled with a tone of derision, a deep guffaw at first that evolved into a high-pitch laugh.

"No, no, of course not," Liddy replied. "But at least I know where my heart lies. With something far more important—with God."

Another customer's loud voice interrupted their conversation. A stout woman in fine clothes, who had been eating at a table nearby, had gone to the counter to confront Mother.

"*Frau* Mittendorf," she spewed out, "what kind of excuse for coffee is this? It's that fake *ersatz* coffee, isn't it? It tastes like roasted chicory, and I won't drink it."

"I'm sorry, *Frau* Heigl," Mother said. "We can't help it. I thought it would be good. In fact, that officer over there in the corner helped us get it." She nodded toward Keppler.

Liddy thought her mother must have figured by connecting it to a man of authority, it would absolve her of any blame, and *Frau* Heigl would accept the explanation.

But the angry woman looked toward Keppler with a sneer. "Big help he's been. Let me tell you where you can get some real coffee. You'll have to pay dearly, but it's not that far from here. I'll write the name of the place for you." She pulled a pad and pen from her purse and brusquely did so, then handed the note to Mother.

"Ah ... thank you," Mother said.

"Good day then!" *Frau* Heigl marched toward the door, but then made a sudden stop in front of Keppler's table.

Oh, no, Liddy thought. *His feathers are already ruffled. He doesn't need anything else right now.*

The two appeared to have a heated conversation, and *Frau* Heigl stormed out.

"Liddy," her mother called. "I've got an errand for you to run."

Thankful to leave the tense situation, Liddy went to the counter where her mother handed her the note.

"Do you know where this place is, Liddy?"

Liddy nodded. "Yes, I do."

"Please go get some real coffee. You had better take your rucksack."

Liddy reached for her rucksack under the counter, but when swinging it onto her shoulder, she dropped the bag, and some of the contents spilled out, including Marek's *mezuzah*. Liddy panicked and hurried to sweep it into her bag, but it was too late.

Keppler had been watching Liddy's every move and observed it all. He almost ran to Liddy's side to check out what he thought he saw. Already in two tangles this morning, he seemed primed for another. He retrieved the *mezuzah*, examining the lettering as he picked it up.

"I know what this is. Who does it belong to?"

"It belongs to a friend of mine," Liddy replied.

"Who is your friend?" Keppler insisted.

"His name is Marek." Her words had come out broken. *Oh, Marek, I hope you've left for the day.*

"Where is he?" Keppler demanded.

Liddy started to glance toward the kitchen but then caught herself. "I'm—I'm not sure."

"*Herr* Keppler," Mother said, "I'll have to ask you to please stop badgering my daughter."

"I need to know where this Marek fellow is," Keppler said.

Liddy's heart sank as Marek, who must have heard his name, came out of the kitchen to face Keppler.

"I'm Marek," he said. "What is the problem, Officer?"

"I've seen you before," Keppler said. "I thought you were a customer. Do you work here?"

In silence, Marek glanced at Mother and Liddy, then looked down.

"Is this yours?" Keppler asked. His impatience furrowed his brow as he held up the *mezuzah*.

"Yes, *mein Herr*."

"Your accent tells me you're not a local German. Let me see your papers. Where are you from?"

"Poland. I'll have to get my papers from my rucksack in the kitchen."

"Get them at once," Keppler demanded.

In seconds, Marek came back and handed Keppler the papers.

Keppler looked at them in disgust. "These are garbage! I know false papers when I see them. I'm saving them as evidence. And I know Hebrew lettering when I see it too. What are you doing with a *mezuzah*? I've seen them on doorposts in the Jewish districts. They're prized possessions."

Liddy gasped. In a flash, the palm of her hand had covered her mouth. *He's Jewish!*

"I had a hunch," Mother whispered to Liddy.

"You're coming with me," Keppler said and grabbed for Marek's arm.

Liddy screamed, "Let him go, *Herr* Keppler. He's done nothing wrong, and we need him here."

"*Herr* Keppler," Mother said, her voice calm, "there must be some mistake. This young man … he comes from a monastery. Why, my Catholic friend tells me she sees him at Mass all the time."

"Well, I'm Catholic, and I've never seen him at Mass," Keppler said. It was clear his patience was wearing thin.

"*Herr* Keppler," Liddy said, "you've told me you've given up your faith. When was the last time you were at Mass?"

"It's none of your business," Keppler growled. "Now get out of my way." He tightened the grip on Marek's arm and looked straight at him. "And *you* are coming with me!"

"I beg you, *Herr* Keppler," Liddy pleaded, "we've been good to you here … because you're a regular customer."

"Besides," Marek said, "that *mezuzah* was given to my family as a gift. I'm a believer in Jesus Christ."

"I've heard that line before from many a Jew trying to save his neck," Keppler said as he pulled Marek toward the door.

"*Herr* Keppler," Mother said, "this young man means no harm. You should remember your own Christian roots and just let him be on his way."

"I'm taking him in. Now stand back."

Marek started to pull away. "You have no grounds to arrest me!" he yelled.

Liddy grabbed Marek's other arm and wouldn't let go. "You can't take him!" she screamed. "Stop, stop!"

"You want to keep harboring a Jew? Then you'll be taken away too," Keppler threatened.

Mother grabbed Liddy's arm and restrained her. "*Herr* Keppler, please," she said. Her breath was ragged, but her demeanor more calm. "It's clear you're giving us no choice here. All I can ask is that you treat him fairly and that God's will be done."

"But Mother, it cannot be God's will that Marek be hauled away!" Liddy said.

"Enough!" Keppler's voice reverberated through the room. "We're done here. He's coming with me." He jerked Marek from Liddy's grasp, bound his hands behind his back with handcuffs, and shoved him out the door.

Liddy collapsed to the floor and wept bitterly. "Oh, Mother, I can't believe what I've just done!"

Chapter 21

Mother reached to help Liddy up off the floor. "Sweetheart, we'll get him back." She pulled her daughter close and hugged her. What had started out as a morning of bad coffee had turned into disaster.

"Where would he be taking Marek?" Liddy asked, her voice still shaking with sobs.

"Most likely to police headquarters for further questioning. Pull yourself together, honey. We've only just begun to fight this."

"I wish Father would get home. He'll know what to do."

"Yes, he should be here any minute. With his connections at the prison, maybe he can do something. I always thought Marek might be Jewish but didn't really want to know, so I was afraid to ask. But I feel worse about being so afraid now." With an unsteady hand, she stroked her hair while she collected her thoughts. "Believe it or not, I actually thought about giving myself up in exchange for Marek like Father Kolbe did in the prison camp." She shook her head in utter dejection as her sad eyes locked on the floor. "After all, I'm a crippled lady—far older than my age. Marek's got his whole life ahead of him. But in the end, I couldn't do it."

Liddy stared at her mother. Loving admiration adorned Liddy's face. "Mother, you really thought of doing that?"

"Well, it did flash through my mind. But I don't think Keppler would have taken me anyway."

The front door opened, and Father walked in. One look at their faces, and he said, "What's happened?"

"Keppler's taken Marek," Liddy blurted. "You've got to help us get him back. Keppler figured out he's Jewish."

"What? How was that?"

"It's all my fault!" A steady stream of tears flooded Liddy's face. "If I had been more careful when I packed that *mezuzah* away, this never would have happened."

Mother slipped her arm around her daughter's shoulders and hugged her again.

"*Mezuzah*? What's that?" Father asked.

"Here it is." She showed her father the *mezuzah*. "I borrowed it from Marek. I was going to show you all but forgot. I never realized a *mezuzah* was a Jewish thing. Marek told me they use it to provide a blessing over their home. It fell out of my bag right in front of Keppler. He then demanded to see Marek's papers and concluded they are fake." Liddy slumped into a chair. "Oh, Father, what are we going to do?"

Mother looked at Father. The look on his face reflected her deep concern.

"I'll contact *Herr* Mueller at the prison," he said. "I'll see if he has any connections, but we must be very careful how we approach this."

"Marek said he's been living with his uncle." Mother watched as Liddy grabbed Marek's rucksack and pulled out all the contents. She laid them on a table: a brooch, a compass, a map, a set of door keys, and a business card. "Here it is," Liddy said. "Marek's uncle's address … and his phone number's on the back."

"What are you going to do?" Father asked.

"I must call him and let him know about Marek." Liddy rushed to the side room to use the phone.

"I worry about our Liddy," Mother said. "This could put her further and further into great danger."

"I know, dear," Father said. "We need to pray in earnest … for both our children."

In seconds, Liddy returned. "There was no answer. But I believe I can find this place on Marek's map. I must go there … at once."

Liddy's father shook his head. "Do you remember the days, Liddy, when you used to be afraid to go out of the house?"

Again Mother's eyes filled with tears, and she gave Liddy a loving hug. "Oh, please be careful, dear Liddy. Please be careful."

****

Riding the bus without Marek was eerie. This time, the seat beside Liddy was empty, except for the rucksack with the map and keys inside. A year had already passed since she had first ventured out with him, amazed then at how busy everyone was with their active lives. But now? How her small world had changed. The ordeal with Keppler haunted her. How could she have been so inept with him? She was so careless to let the *mezuzah* tumble out of her rucksack. Then so emotional. Why had she failed to reason with him more about Marek's Catholic connections?

Twenty minutes later, she arrived at the address on Rosenberg's card. Before her stood a stately apartment building that had thus far escaped the cruelties of war. *So this is where Marek has lived all this time.*

Liddy went up two flights of stairs and knocked on a door, but there was no answer. She knocked again, this time louder, and waited. Still no answer. Liddy had Marek's keys, but she could not bring herself to reach for them in his rucksack. Had she not chastised her father for snooping? But this was different. It was a life-and-death situation, was it not?

Liddy pulled the keys from her sack and tried each of three keys until one finally fit. She turned it slowly until the bolt released. She opened the door a crack. Her soft voice called out: "Hello? Is anybody here?"

With no response, Liddy snuck into the room. She spotted several pieces of unopened mail on a table and picked up a few envelopes, all addressed to a "Friedrich Reimer." Panic-stricken, she dropped them, and her eyes darted around the room. Was she in the wrong place? She searched for anything that might be familiar, relieved at last to spot what looked like one of Marek's caps on another table in a far corner. Her curiosity compelled her to continue her search.

Liddy opened a bedroom door and came across some spartan furniture. *This must be his room.* A number of clothing items were strewn on the floor, including one of Marek's shirts. She inched toward a walk-in closet with its door a tad ajar. A rustling noise in the back of the closet startled her.

Liddy screamed and slammed the door shut. "Is someone in there?" She backed away.

More shuffling noises from the closet. *Could it just be the cat?*

"Anyone in there?" Liddy asked again.

A slender girl emerged—the one with the short-cropped hair Marek knew at the print shop.

"You're Anna," Liddy said. "You delivered the envelope for Marek. What are you doing hiding in there?"

"I thought the police were coming for me."

"Oh, dear. I'm Marek's friend … from the bakery." Liddy's heart sank with negative thoughts. "Are you Marek's girlfriend?"

"Oh, no. I'm Marek's cousin. My mother died some time ago. I live here with my father."

"I noticed some mail on the table. Why aren't the envelopes addressed to Saul Rosenberg?"

"He had to change his name a long time ago. But I haven't seen him for two days now. I'm afraid he was taken away by the Gestapo." Her voice carried an overriding desperation. "I thought they were coming for me when I heard you at the door. Thank God, it's just you. But what are you doing here?"

"I need to find Marek's uncle to tell him the police took Marek away."

Fear draped Anna's face. "They've taken Marek too?"

"Yes, and your father has disappeared?"

"Yes. I wasn't here when it happened. He wasn't planning to go out, so the Gestapo must have come here. He's probably on some train to purgatory." Anna's eyes welled up, and tears trickled down her thin face.

"You mean to a concentration camp?"

"Don't say those words, I shudder at the thought." Sobbing soon revealed her inner pain.

"Oh, Anna." Liddy wrapped her arms around the girl. "I wish we could do something Now I understand why you had removed that star from your shirt. So you're Jewish, and Marek is—?"

"His mother was Jewish. His father was Catholic."

Chapter 22

Oh, dear God, I so want to make things different. Liddy pulled the bedcovers farther over her head. It was Tuesday right after dinner and hours before her normal bedtime. *How could I have been so careless?* Curling up into a ball, she felt like a worthless lump of stale dough. *Just toss me in the trash. Surely God forgot the yeast when He made me! What am I good for anyway?* She trembled in fear, wild pounding overtook her heart, and a barrage of tears flowed down her face.

She so wanted to see Marek. *But would it ever happen again? Oh, dear God, please ... even if it's just one last time. But would Marek turn away, too disgusted to even face me? Would he just shake his head at me? Would God? Why should I even go on living?* A knock on the door startled her.

"Come out here, Liddy Mittendorf," commanded her father's stern voice. "You can't keep moping about Marek."

"I'm in no mood to talk about it, Father. Please go away."

"No, I'm not going away. You need to pull yourself together. Now, please let me in." Father's last few words turned compassionate—a tone she had not heard from him in quite some time.

Liddy dragged herself out of bed and unlocked the door.

Father gazed into her eyes, the same love in his voice also in his eyes. "You must stop torturing yourself, Liddy. What's done is done."

"I know, but I just can't forgive myself. If I had stayed in my room that morning, like I am now, Marek would be a free man. I didn't keep the *mezuzah* safe. And then I said, 'So you *are* Jewish.' That sealed his future right there. It's all my fault."

"Yes, I can see how that troubles you. But sometimes things just happen."

"I feel like such a failure and not the person God wants me to be. Even *Herr* Bonhoeffer said a person has to start with discipline."

"But do you think God loves you any less than He did last week?"

"Probably! I wouldn't blame Him. I don't deserve His love."

"So then what? Each time you fall short, you feel a little less loved? At some point, you'd feel like God has forsaken you altogether. Don't we know someone who already said those words?"

"You mean Jesus on the cross?" She softly mouthed out the words, "My God, my God—why hast Thou forsaken Me?"

"Yes, but we know it was already part of God's plan. He would sacrifice His only son. For us, the full price has been paid. Now we are the ones who should never have to ask that question again." Father put his arms around Liddy and hugged her. His tight squeeze felt so reassuring. "Always remember, *meine Liebschen*, just because you're not the person you want to be doesn't mean God loves you any less. You may feel you've made a huge mistake, but that doesn't matter. You are already forgiven by Jesus on the cross. God's love is unconditional—available to us all everywhere—if we just truly believe it."

"I think it must have been God's love coming out through Mother the other day when Keppler arrested Marek. She told you what she thought about doing, didn't she?"

Klaus shook his head.

"No? This surprised me when I heard about it. Mother actually thought about telling Keppler to take her instead of Marek."

"What?" He looked stunned and moved to sit down on Liddy's bed. "Say that again."

In a more measured voice, Liddy repeated, "Mother considered telling Keppler to take her instead of Marek."

Klaus shook his head again. "Sometimes I realize I really don't know my wife. I would never have thought that her mind would go there. That's amazing."

Liddy sat beside her father and slipped her arm around his shoulders as he wrapped his arm around her waist. For several moments, they sat in silence while Liddy's mind replayed the awful scene with Keppler and Marek one more time.

At last, Father spoke. "Liddy Mittendorf, you would be so much happier … more content … if you would listen better to God."

"What do you mean?"

"Why don't you believe, once and for all, how much God loves you—right now? When you understand the full magnitude of it, the best part comes later."

"How's that?"

"When you really feel loved, you don't worry so much about the consequences of things. You'll be amazed at how free from fear you'll feel, and how easy it is to pass that love on. Trust me. Better yet, trust God."

"I'll try, Father. I promise I will. But, oh, I do worry about God's plan for Marek. I'm afraid I might never see him again."

"But that doesn't mean you can't keep trying. Your efforts still matter. They may all be a part of God's plan."

"You're right, Father. There's more I could do." Liddy paused another moment. She pulled on her sleeves and smoothed her blouse. "I know what I'm going to do. Since Keppler stopped coming here, I'll go to him."

****

"I'm going to see Keppler," Liddy informed Mother at lunch the next day.

"You're going to do what?" Mother asked as she almost choked on her bread.

"I'm going to see Keppler," Liddy replied. She continued to pack a few small pastries in her rucksack.

"Now think this through, Liddy. Are you sure you want to subject yourself to that man? He is very, very powerful. I don't want you to do it."

Mother's words sank into Liddy's heart like a sharp knife. She stopped packing, then walked to her chair and sat down. Her shoulders drooped from the magnitude of those comments. "You're right, Mother. I'm no match for Keppler ..." She began to weep and bowed her head to pray.

"I'm glad you've come to your senses," her mother said. She reached to give her a quick hug.

But Liddy then stood again, and said, "No, Mother ... I really must go. I feel I owe it to Marek. He has tremendous courage. I don't think it's asking too much for me to try to help." She finished packing.

"Well then, if you feel God wants you to do something, so be it.

Why do you pack that sack of baked goods?"

"I made a fresh streusel cake this morning to take to Keppler … if I can find him. I made it with extra sugar. I've also packed an *M* signature loaf. Mother, please tell me you'll pray for me."

"My prayers … and my heart … are always with you, Liddy. God will be with you."

****

The thin female clerk wore a gray-green uniform similar to Keppler's but less ornate. Liddy guessed the woman was about as old as her mother. Liddy scrutinized her thin blonde hair pulled straight back into a bun and wire-rimmed glasses that framed her angular face—a face already showing mid-afternoon weariness. The woman peered over the top of her glasses as Liddy approached the desk. The glare of a single lamp reflected off a stack of white papers. "Yes?" came the question, so cold that it sent nervous chills up Liddy's back.

"Is *Herr* Keppler here?" squeaked out from Liddy's mouth.

"Yes, he's always back here by 3:30," said the woman with a strong, commanding tone. "Who is calling?"

"My name is Liddy Mittendorf. He knows me." She tried to stand erect and dared to probe straight into the woman's glaring eyes. The clerk stared back at Liddy while she picked up the phone. She asked for *Herr* Keppler, but soon hung up, and said, "He's busy with someone and can't see you right now."

"I'll wait."

"It could take hours," the woman said. Her monotone voice revealed to Liddy she didn't care how long it took.

"I'll wait," Liddy repeated then sat on a hard, wooden chair in a dark corner. Except for her, no one else occupied any of the other chairs lined up against the three bare gray walls.

Liddy's thoughts drifted to Marek. Could he be here in this very building, locked up in a cell a few walls away? She dreaded the thought that he might already be at a work camp. Oh, how she hoped he was still here. Could he sense her presence? Perhaps he had an extra beat of joy in his heart today, in hopes that she was somewhere fighting for him? With her mind so occupied with the thoughts of Marek and the past week, almost thirty minutes passed.

Another officer came in, hustled past Liddy, entered another room behind the clerk, and slammed the door. His smelly cigar clouded the already dank room and distracted Liddy for a moment. She glanced at the wall clock. *More than a half hour has passed. I'll check again.* "Perhaps *Herr* Keppler is free now?" she asked the clerk. But a second call produced the same results.

"May I leave him a note?" Liddy almost demanded.

"Yes," the clerk said and handed over a piece of paper and a pen.

Liddy wrote a personal plea to release Marek and pulled out the baked goods. "Do you have a piece of tape? It's very important. I want to make sure that Herr Keppler gets these together."

As Liddy taped the note to the package, the door behind the clerk opened. A thin man with disheveled hair sheepishly approached the clerk and gave her a handful of papers. His ragged appearance, bruises on his face and arms, and a forlorn look exuded fear and apprehension … yet a twinge of hope. A prisoner being released!

"Excuse me, *mein Herr*," Liddy said. "May I ask if anyone else is being released?

"I-I wouldn't know." The man's voice quivered. "I-I didn't see anyone being processed. They told me I could go just in the last few minutes—not enough evidence."

"What were—?"

"Enough!" the clerk raised her voice as she examined the man's papers and stamped them. "You," she pointed at Liddy with an accusing finger, "get out of here. It's none of your business what happens to anyone in this place." She shoved the papers into the man's chest and said, "And you get out too … before we change our minds."

The man hurried outside with Liddy following right on his heels. When they had walked several meters away from the building, the man turned toward her. "What did you want to know?" he whispered.

"*Mein Herr*," she said, "why were you arrested?"

"Political subversion. The Nazi Youth raided Pharus Hall, where there is a lot of political talk. I'm a musician with the Swing Kids."

"I've been there and danced to your music. I was there when the Nazi Youth raided the place." She scanned her surroundings and lowered her voice. "Thank God, Marek and I managed to get away. You haven't seen another prisoner who looks kind of like you but younger?"

"No, I haven't. I'm one of the lucky ones. It's a good thing I had some musical connections. I think he liked me because of that."

"Who is *he*? Is his name Keppler?"

"Yes!" Surprise splashed all over the man's face. "How do you know him?"

"Let's just say I do know about him … unfortunately."

"When he released me, he said not to leave before telling the *Fräulein* that I was his Barabbas for the day."

Chapter 23

L iddy arrived back at the bakery later Wednesday afternoon. Still disturbed by the events at the police station, she stormed through the front door. Her mother watched her every step—anxious to hear the results of the visit to see Keppler.

"That man is going to drive me crazy! He's taunting me, Mother. I can't believe it." She paced back and forth.

"What happened?" Mother stopped kneading bread dough, wiped her brow, and stared at her daughter.

"Keppler wouldn't release Marek—there was no sign of him. Keppler released Barabbas instead!"

"Barabbas? What are you talking about, Liddy?"

"He released a different prisoner—a musician. He sent him out the front door—right past my very eyes—I think just to make sure I saw the man. You know, Keppler is probably well versed in the Christian beliefs. The problem is he's on the wrong side of them now. I wish I could fix that!" She raised her arms in frustration.

"I would hardly equate Marek with Jesus Christ," Mother said. She paused then added, "Except that he's Jewish."

"Of course not, Mother. Don't be silly—I'm not doing that. But now I understand how all those followers of Jesus must have felt when Barabbas was released. Can you imagine that? They desperately hoped and prayed for Jesus to get released—only to get Barabbas? My stomach is a hollow pit right now."

"I know it's hard to imagine. But, my dear Liddy, instead of Jesus, you know the people clamored for Barabbas. That's how it was all meant to be."

Liddy's eyes grew moist. She shook her head in disbelief. "Mother, are you saying it is meant to be that I should never see Marek again?"

"We don't know that yet, do we? Let's see how God's plan unfolds. I'm so sorry—really I am. I know how much you wanted to see Marek. Maybe, like you say, Keppler's plan is only to toy with you, and he'll stop by the bakery in a day or two."

"Do you just say that to make me feel better?" She slumped at a table and hung her head. "The worst part is I just don't know. I dread having to wait. The guilt still eats away at me. Maybe Father has made some headway with his connections. Is he still in bed?"

"Yes. He should be up soon. But let's focus on something more positive. Do you remember what happens tomorrow?"

"With everything going on with Marek, I almost forgot. Willy's due home tomorrow."

"Yes. We've received word he should arrive at the bus station about 7:30 in the evening. Your father can get him before work."

"I have indeed missed Willy. Maybe some glorious notes from his piano will take my mind off my troubles."

****

Long after dark, just before Father headed off to work, someone knocked at the front door.

"Why would someone be calling on the Mittendorfs this late?" mused Father as he made his way to the door. Liddy and Mother watched from the doorway of the side room.

A female voice in the shadows said, "Please, *Herr* Mittendorf, may I come in?"

"Yes, please do," Father replied in a cautious tone.

Liddy studied the doorway as a young lady with a dilapidated suitcase stepped inside. It was Anna!

"Anna, what are you doing here?" Liddy hurried to greet her.

"Hello, Liddy. I couldn't stay at my home any longer. It's too dangerous."

"Father, Mother," Liddy said, "this is Marek's cousin Anna Rosenberg. No, now it's Anna Reimer."

"I see," Father said, still with a bit of reservation. "So you're another one who's part of the resistance."

Mother joined the group and greeted the visitor. "Such a shame you have to sneak about in the dark, my dear."

"I'm sorry, I have no other place to go," Anna said. "But I don't want to endanger you either. I don't know what to do. Could I stay just a night or two?"

Father looked at Mother then at Anna. "Well, we would feel bad if we had to put you back out on the street, but … just a moment. I need to discuss this with my family."

While Anna waited, Father, Mother, and Liddy moved to the other side of the room at Father's request.

Liddy jumped in with a few choice words. "There's no way we can do anything but keep Anna here. Right, Mother?"

"Well, I don't know, Liddy. Aren't we in enough trouble with Keppler already?"

Liddy stared at her father, who looked down, his shoulders slumped, his brow furrowed with the deep creases of another tough decision he had to make.

"Do you realize what this could mean for us?" he asked. "Maybe the end of the bakery that we've worked so hard to save. Renate, you're right. They've already got us on their blacklist. We could all be taken away." He looked up. "Dear Lord," he prayed, "give me the right words."

Liddy and Mother also prayed, asking God for wisdom to know what to do.

Mother whispered, "Klaus, maybe we should help her ... just tonight."

Father walked back to Anna. Mother and Liddy followed.

"We want to help you," he said. "You're welcome to stay as long as you need. You can sleep in Willy's bed tonight, and until we can make other arrangements, in Liddy's room. Of course, you're going to have to stay out of sight during the day."

"I don't know how I can thank you enough. Truly—I mean it from the bottom of my heart. God bless you!"

In the midst of all the turmoil, Liddy's heart felt a rare moment of peace.

****

The following morning, Liddy woke up with a new resolve. She would no longer wait to hear from Keppler. She must go see him again, but this time, she was determined not to warm the seat of a waiting room chair.

As she approached the police station that afternoon, she looked at her watch, the one *Grossmutter* had given her for Christmas a few years back. Always one to encourage Liddy to reach outside her shell, *Grossmutter* would no doubt be proud of what she was about to do. At precisely 3:30, the time by which the clerk had said *Herr* Keppler was always there, Liddy marched through the door with another package of baked goods and asked to see him.

"I'll check," the same clerk said with the same follow-up: "He's not available at this time."

Liddy took a deep breath, prayed for courage, and started to walk toward the door behind the clerk. "*Herr* Keppler knows me. I'm delivering a personal package for him."

"Wait, *Fräulein!*"

"Don't worry. I'll be right back," was her reply, partially eclipsed by the sound of the door closing behind her.

Liddy hurried down a long hallway. She viewed a number of small offices in a row, all with opened doors and men in uniforms working at desks. As she walked past the doors, a few heads looked up at her in surprise, one of them Keppler! She stopped and stood her ground in his doorway.

"What are you doing here?" he yelled, slamming his pencil down on a stack of papers. He sat behind a dark-gray desk, where another neatly stacked pile of papers seemed to vie for his attention. With the small cramped space that Keppler had, Liddy surmised this was no man of insurmountable power. He would not hide behind the trappings of authority if she had anything to do with it.

Just then, someone grabbed Liddy's arm from behind.

"I'm sorry, *Herr* Keppler," the clerk said as she pulled Liddy toward her. "She slipped past me. It won't happen again." The clerk started down the hallway, dragging Liddy with her. "You come with me … now!" she demanded.

"Wait!" Keppler yelled, then appeared in his doorway. "It's all right. I'll see her if she's that determined."

"Yes, *Herr* Keppler," the clerk said. She released Liddy, hurried down the hallway, and slammed the door.

"Now," Keppler growled at Liddy, "what's so critical that you have to disturb my important work for the *Führer?*" He motioned for her to come into his office and closed the door behind them.

"*Herr* Keppler, did you get my other note? I wanted to give you these treats and implore you to release Marek." She held up her package. "These are made with his recipes. He's a good person who just wants to make Germany a better place."

"Listen, *Fräulein,* save your breath. For all I know, he may already be shipped out."

"He's already gone?"

"I suspect so."

"Please don't tell me that, *Herr* Keppler!"

"We determined he's at least half Jewish—a *Tauscher*. He's subject to all the rules and regulations that we are bound to enforce," he said in a matter-of-fact way.

"But it's not too late to do something, is it?"

Keppler hesitated. "I don't know … nor should I care."

Liddy paused, then said, "*Herr* Keppler, you told us that your Christian faith was once important to you. May I remind you that Jesus was a Jew as well? And what about Mendelsohn? I heard you say he's your favorite composer. I remember studying him in school—he was Jewish."

"Don't start down that path, *Fräulein.* I warn you. Now you need to leave. I am busy."

"But, *mein Herr,*" She grabbed his arm. "Please don't abandon the teachings of the Bible. Rise above all this hatred of the Jews!"

"Enough!" he yelled.

"I implore you, *Herr* Keppler. Be a real man. Be a Christian man."

Keppler glared at Liddy, his knuckles white as he held a clenched fist in front of her face. "Get out now, before I lock you up for harboring a Jew!"

Liddy took a step back, but a surge of courage enabled her to speak. "All right, I'll go. But when you eat these, maybe you'll do it in remembrance of Marek." Liddy shoved the package into Keppler's chest, turned, and started down the hallway. But then she stopped and looked at Keppler one more time. "Remember, *Herr* Keppler. God loves you too."

Keppler stood in silence, his face troubled.

"Wait, *Fräulein!*"

Liddy stopped and stared at Keppler … waiting.

Keppler's eyes fixed on Liddy's. His lips twitched as the words struggled to get out. "God loves me? Even," he said, then cleared his throat. "Even if I, a man who prides himself on his precision, forgets to give his dying brother his medications?"

"Of course." Taken aback by hearing such a personal revelation from the man, Liddy took several steps toward him and smiled. "You may have given up on God, but He's not going to forsake you."

Keppler just stood, staring at her. For the first time, she noticed his eyes turn glassy with emotion.

She turned to leave again but lingered when he mumbled something barely audible. "I played the piano for him for hours. He loved it." But just as she felt she may have connected with his soul, it all changed. In an instant, his eyes turned steely again. It was as if he had just rushed to the front line to thwart an attack and was back on the offensive. "*Fräulein*, I have another question for you. Am I loved even if Marek was shipped off to a work camp?"

Keppler's question caught Liddy completely off guard. The ball of energy that she had become deflated in an instant. Her quivering lips struggled to form the words. "Yes, *Herr* Keppler— God might be angry with you, but He would still love you. It's called unconditional love."

Keppler remained pensive for a moment. "But what about you, *Fräulein?* Would you ..." Again the words seemed trapped. "Would you forgive me?"

Liddy's face flushed red-hot. "Is this some sort of game you're playing?"

An all-knowing glint flashed in his eyes, and a rock-solid steadiness returned to his jaw. "No, *Fraulein*. I just want us both to be honest with ourselves."

Liddy's eyes filled with a flood of tears. "Yes, *Herr* Keppler, you can choose to be a person who is angry at God all the time—who plays these little games of 'why' or 'why not.' As for me, I choose to focus on God's love and forgiveness. That's what my faith is all about."

Chapter 24

Keppler rolled over one more time early Friday morning and gazed at the clock. He struggled to get his mind to register on the small hour hand. Was it just past the four, or was it the five? The minute hand seemed to be at thirty-seven. *Oh well, what does it matter? Forget about trying to get back to sleep—better resign myself to getting up and out of bed.*

After he completed his morning routine in the bathroom, he returned to the chair by his bedside to examine the uniform he had laid out the night before. He bent over to smooth out a few remaining wrinkles. It was a uniform he would wear with great distinction this day. Yes, indeed, he was a patriot. No one could deny him that. He began to dress.

His uniform on, Keppler rubbed his eyes as he stood in front of the mirror. Oh, how he wished he had slept better. It was mornings like this when his body was weary, that his musical background seemed to take over. Poetic verses syncopated in his head as if his mind were intent on writing the stanzas to a musical piece.

Why so unsettled? 'Twas a dreadful night!

Pull that belt in—another notch, yes, tight.

Who is this *Fräulein* who challenges me so?

Polish those buttons—the brass needs to glow.

Why do I let her have such power over me? After all, I'm Conrad Keppler, officer extraordinaire. She's only a young *Fräulein* who peddles tasteless pastries and pours bad coffee. That is, when she's not talking about her faith and her God. Just try getting her to stop.

I once knew my God, but then I hit bottom;

Losing a brother, then wife, was too much to fathom.

Let it go, dear *Fräulein*! Please, why do you care?

I was fixed on being mad—as mad as I could bear.

And what about that Marek fellow? Appears to be a decent lad. But he's Jewish. The rules say he must be shipped off to a work camp. No doubt about it. Yes, the *Fraulein's* fought the good fight for him. Her heart seems broken; her eyes are so sad. But this is a war we are waging; she's got to toughen up! Let him go, *Fräulein*!

But, oh my, do I wonder—just who is she?

A *Fräulein* who'd forgive me; just how can that be?

So is it true there is a love that transcends?

With no more worries about making amends?

Forgiveness she knows; so perhaps I should too;

How 'bout the God I once loved. "Yes, why not You?"

Well, I'm Conrad Keppler—there'll be a day I die.

The face of God she'll see. But, alas, will I?

****

Liddy sat at the dinner table that evening with mixed feelings. Mother and Father's talk all centered on Willy coming home that very night. Yes, she was excited about that, but what about Marek? Everyone seemed to be avoiding the subject. Anna had also joined them, holding her audience captive with her stories about her background. But Liddy only half listened, worrying about whether Marek had been shipped out.

"Anna, we have to figure out how we're going to hide you if the time comes," Father said.

"I'm good at finding creative places," Anna replied.

"Like what?" Father asked.

"Like under some planks over a hole in the cellar. Of course, it would have to look inconspicuous."

"We don't have anything like that now, but perhaps I could fix something," Father said.

"Father's ingenious when it comes to building and making things," Liddy said. "He'll come up with something that will work. Ma-Marek would have been of great help too." She choked on her words and her eyes misted.

"In the meantime," Mother said, "there's a closet downstairs. You'll have to make friends with the onions and root vegetables, but that's the best we can do right now. Remember to always use the back stairway. It's a good thing we have that."

"Yes, that's something I learned from *Frau* Von Thadden years ago at her boarding school—always use all the resources available to you," Anna said.

Liddy did a double-take as she tuned back into the conversation. "You went to *Frau* Von Thadden's boarding school?" she asked. "I've met her. It was just last year—a very nice woman. When did you go to her school?"

"About five years ago, well before the war," Anna replied. "My father was a successful businessman back then and wanted me to get the best education." Her eyes began to fill with tears. "That was horrible news about her, wasn't it?"

"What news? What happened?" Liddy nervously chewed on her lip.

Anna paused as she seemed to struggle with a lump in her throat. "She appeared last week before the People's Court."

"And?"

"She was sentenced to death for treason."

Liddy and Mother gasped.

Everyone at the table sat stunned, staring at each other. Tears flowed freely down Liddy's cheeks. The news about *Frau* Van Thadden drove her emotions wild while everyone sat in abject silence.

"Our earnest prayers are more important than ever during this time of evil," Mother said.

"Yes, let us never forget that." Father glanced at his watch, and a surprised look marked his face. "Oh, I've got to head to the bus station for Willy right now." He grabbed one last bite of his dinner and got up from the table.

Liddy glanced at her mother, the only one who smiled at Father's words about Willy, no doubt music to her ears.

To Liddy's chagrin, *Frau* Von Thadden's funeral march was the only music that played in her head. But what sort of music would follow for Marek?

Chapter 25

The phone rang later that evening, and Mother answered it. Liddy, at work in the kitchen, listened as her mother spoke: "Oh, don't tell me that, Klaus. You should have checked before you left. Yes, I know you still have to work tonight, but what else are we going to do? You'll have to wait there until he arrives. Okay. Good-bye."

As her mother entered the kitchen, disappointment came through clearly in her voice. "Willy's bus has had a mechanical breakdown. Now they say it's going to be at least a couple of hours late."

"Oh no," Liddy said. "I'm sure Willy's not happy about that."

"I should say not. But nobody can be any unhappier than I am right now," Mother said.

Liddy finished drying a stack of clean dinner dishes. "That reminds me of the time when we all left on a bus for the trip to *Grossmutter* and *Grossvater's* in Munich. Remember? The bus broke down, and after about thirty minutes, Willy had that terrible tantrum in front of all those people. We were all stuck together in that confined space. I don't know if anyone else thought it was amusing, but as for me at my age, I was so embarrassed. But then, he was only about six at the time." She paused to reminisce. "All in all, though, those were pretty good years, I must say. I miss them."

"Yes, any time before the war was good," Mother replied.

Still in deep thought, Liddy said, "Willy kind of reminds me of Marek—always wants to move forward. Speaking of Marek, it doesn't look like Father has made any headway with his contacts."

"No, I guess not." Mother fidgeted with the sleeve of her dress. "Oh, Liddy, I'd better be straight with you. Until now, I haven't had the heart. They told your father they couldn't do anything about it. When they started to ask a lot of questions, he figured it was best to drop it."

Liddy looked down and shook her head. "I was afraid that was the case. But I wish *Herr* Keppler would get back to me. I thought we were starting to connect. I need to do something to get my mind off all this trouble." She went into the side room to grab a book from a shelf, then flopped on the sofa. After a moment, she tossed the book aside. "This isn't going to work. I'm going to the church to sort clothes for next Saturday's drive."

"At this time of day?" her mother asked. "You'll have to come home in the dark."

"I could get to church and back in my sleep, Mother. Don't worry about me."

****

A few hours later, Renate had settled into her favorite chair while she read under the light of the single lamp in the side room. In accordance with the rules, the shades had been drawn tight to keep any light from seeping into the dark night.

When she checked the time, she told herself, "Klaus and Willy should come walking through our front door any minute. Or, at least, they should've called. And where's Liddy? She should be back by now."

A noise outside the door then raised her hopes. She heard a loud knock and got up to answer.

"Coming! I'll be right there," she yelled, then reached to open the door. There, with a big smile across his face stood Marek. He carried a large bag on his shoulder.

"Oh, Marek! Come in! Come in!"

When he stepped inside, Renate gave him a warm embrace, then called out for Anna upstairs, "Anna! Marek is here."

"This is quite the welcome, *Frau* Mittendorf. How things have changed. You know there was a time when I felt like a wad of dough you never trusted to rise."

"Of course, we're so happy to have you back. We thought you had been sent away." Anna rushed down the stairs and into the front room and gave Marek a huge hug.

"What are *you* doing here?" Marek asked, but did not wait for an answer. "Where's Liddy?" he quickly followed with a disappointed look on his face. "I was really looking forward to seeing her."

"She's at church sorting clothes. She should be home any minute," Renate said. "As well as Klaus with Willy. This just might be one grand reunion." With the weight of the war's burdens lifted at that moment from Renate's heart, she discovered newfound energy.

"Oh, Marek, it's so good to see you," Anna said. "What's happened to you?"

"It's a long story," Marek said.

"You're looking well," Anna continued. "I'm surprised, considering what you've been through. What happened? How did you get released?"

"Keppler had a change of heart."

"Come—let's all sit down," Renate said. "I'm anxious to hear it." She eased herself onto the sofa.

"I'd really like for Liddy to hear this too," Marek said. "Could we please call her and see if she's still at the church?"

"Of course." Renate reached for the phone and called, but there was no answer. "She must be in the church basement." Her worry soon faded, replaced by intrigue about Marek. "Come on. We can't wait! Please tell us. And what's in the bag?"

"Yes, Marek, we want all the details," Anna echoed.

"I'm so glad Liddy left that note for Keppler at the station and brought those baked treats for him," Marek said with a wide smile.

"Just because of them?" Renate asked with a twinge of skepticism. "I know she added extra sugar, but—"

Marek laughed. "Really, sugar has nothing to do with it. There's an interesting story behind all that. It dawned on me not long ago, and I've never had a chance to tell any of you. At Father Kolbe's monastery, we printed a newspaper that went to thousands of Catholics around the world. Guess who used to be one of the steady readers? Before he drifted away from his faith, that is." He paused before giving his answer: "Keppler. Can you believe it?"

"I still don't understand," Renate said.

"In the upper left-hand corner of every newspaper, Father Kolbe printed a special *M* logo to honor Mary. I didn't realize it, but my mind made almost a precise copy of that logo when I created the signature loaves. It was unique, with such a long flourish at the end. Keppler's mind finally made the connection. It was enough for him to believe my monastery story."

"So he released you just like that?" Renate asked, her eyes wide.

"No, it wasn't that simple. He came back to the station after his shift—it was well after dark. He told me all about why he had changed his mind. He opened the cell door, and I stepped right out. But then the strangest thing happened. Keppler lingered inside."

"Lingered inside?" Renate's brow furrowed.

"Yes, that powerful man sat on the bed shaking his head and muttering to himself as if *he* were the one worthy of conviction. I had always thought of him as being so strong. At that moment, his resigned face turned angelic. I finally asked, 'Can we go, *Herr* Keppler?'

"At last, he escorted me out. We walked right past the night guard, but all of a sudden we heard a 'Halt!' The guard asked for the authorization papers signed by the Kommandant. Keppler casually pulled some folded papers out of his coat pocket and flashed them at the guard. The guard must have been too tired to examine them. I noticed some signatures on the papers, but I suspect they were fake—even I could have done a better job drumming up those documents." Marek chuckled. His words flowed easily as he basked in his newfound freedom. "Now I'm a free man. Oh, and he also gave me some things to give to Willy and Liddy."

Renate struggled to make sense of Marek's story. "Even though your father was Catholic, you're part Jewish, Marek. Why didn't you tell us, or at least Liddy?"

"I was afraid that once you knew, you might feel obligated to report me."

"But Keppler could have still kept you, right?"

"Yes, I know, but he seemed intent to overlook that. In the end, it was Liddy fighting for me that made the difference. Keppler told me all about what she did. He said she brought a new focus to him of what's important. He'd been angry at God, but she reminded him of the faith he once had. And it wasn't just the words—she was brave the way she demonstrated her faith. What can I say? She's an amazing girl."

"You know what this means," Renate said. "Keppler has finally decided to put God above his country. Hallelujah!" She raised her hands high in jubilation but then grimaced in pain due to her physical limitations. It was a small reminder, too, that even a victory salute must pay homage to all the inescapable struggles that are part of the journey.

"Praise God," Marek said. "Keppler also gave me a special message for Liddy, but I want to tell her face-to-face."

"Oh, Marek, please share it with us now. We won't tell her."

"All right. He said to be sure to thank the *Fräulein* and tell her congratulations on her hard-fought victory. He said she had won the battle, but, then, she didn't fight fair."

"How so?"

"She had God on her side."

The three of them laughed and relished the unbelievable change in events.

"We really need to join together in a prayer of thanks," Marek added.

No sooner had those words come from his mouth, than the most unwelcome wail of an air-raid siren shattered their sense of peace and well-being.

"I can't believe it. Not this, not now," Renate exclaimed. "And Liddy's ... I hope she's safe in the church."

"We'll trust she'll be safe," Marek said. "Let's get downstairs. I think we've got this routine down pretty good by now."

"Yes, we must hurry," Renate said. "Anna, turn out all the lights and hurry to the cellar with us."

****

In the cellar, Renate glanced at Marek, still holding the bag that Keppler had given to him for Willy and Liddy.

"Please, Marek," Renate said, "tell us what's in that bag."

"I'm not sure myself." Marek reached in and pulled out two shirts. "Ah, I know what these are for." He read a note Keppler had pinned to one of them. "It says, 'For Liddy's next clothing drive— they're clean.'" Marek chuckled. "Then there's also an envelope in here marked for Willy."

"Please read it to us," Renate said.

Marek opened the envelope and positioned the flashlight directly over it. "This is incredible. It's a page from the newspaper we used to print at Father Kolbe's monastery, *The Knight*. Keppler must have saved these issues going way back."

"Knowing him, that doesn't surprise me," Renate said.

"Oh, look—right here is the *M* logo I just told you about." Marek held up the page for Renate and Anna. "See? Doesn't that look a lot like the top of the signature loaf?" Marek examined the page further. "Why, it's an article all about the origins of 'Ave Maria' and the different words that have been associated with it. Liddy told me Willy was quite anxious to get them." He read aloud:

"Ave Maria" by Franz Schubert

Hail Mary, full of grace, the Lord is with Thee.

Blessed art Thou among women,

And blessed is the fruit of Thy womb, Jesus.

Holy Mary, Mother of God

Pray for us sinners,

Now and in the hour of our death. Amen.

"The music is so beautiful," Renate said. "It's easy to overlook the words, but it's not complete without them."

The all-clear siren blasted, and Renate released a long sigh. "Thank God, we made it through another one."

In minutes, they all had climbed their way upstairs, for Renate much easier than the trek down. Some time later, the phone rang, and they rushed to the side room.

"Oh, dear Lord, please let it be Klaus or Liddy," Renate said, picking up the phone. "Hello? Are you still at the bus station?" Her hand slammed against her forehead. "There must be some mistake. Are you sure? No, Klaus!" She hung up and screamed, "God help him!"

"What is it?" Marek and Anna asked in unison.

"My poor Willy," Renate sobbed. "A bomb has hit his bus!"

Chapter 26

"What are we going to do?" Renate sobbed.

"Come sit down, *Frau* Mittendorf," Marek said as he slipped his arm around the woman's waist. "We've got to think this through."

"Yes," she said as she collapsed on the sofa. "I can't think straight. That last line of the words to 'Ave Maria' is so haunting, 'Now and in the hour of our death.' I can't bear to think of my Willy, the youngest of us all." She burst into deep, agonizing sobs.

"*Frau* Mittendorf, that line is foreshadowing for all of us. We don't know when our time will come. But, at least, we already know Jesus when the hour strikes. Let's pull ourselves together and figure out what to do." He paused and sat next to Renate while Anna sat in a nearby chair.

"Did *Herr* Mittendorf say where the bus is?" Anna asked.

Deep in thought, Renate rubbed her forehead. "He said in the Weissensee District near the park lake."

"Let me get my map," Marek said. He retrieved the map from his rucksack, opened it, and pointed at the paper. "Here it is," he said and showed Renate. Anna came to Renate's side and looked at the map.

"What can we do?" Anna asked.

Renate reached for the telephone. "I've got to try to contact Liddy again." She let the phone ring and ring at the church and hoped and prayed for an answer. Much to her relief, Liddy picked up on the other end.

"Oh, Liddy. I'm so glad to hear your voice. Are you all right?"

"Yes, Mother," Liddy said. "There was no damage to the church."

"Liddy, listen. Your father called—a terrible thing has happened." Renate sobbed.

"What's happened?"

"Willy's bus has been hit by a bomb. I pray, dear God, that he's … he's—" Renate broke down again.

"Oh, Mother, how horrible. What about Father? Is he all right?"

"Yes, he was not hurt, but we must pray for Willy."

"Where did this happen?" Liddy asked.

"Your father said it was in the Weissensee District near the park lake."

The phone went dead on the other end. "Liddy? Liddy!"

"She hung up," Renate said to Marek and Anna. "She must have left for the bomb site."

"That sounds like the new Liddy," Marek said. "But you didn't have the chance to tell her that Keppler had released me." With a determined look, he rose to leave. "I'm going to meet her there."

"Marek, no," Renate said. "You shouldn't risk it. Police will be there. You're staying here with us. Please."

Marek stood in deep thought. But soon he said, "I'm sorry, *Frau* Mittendorf. I need to be there with Liddy. She'll be the first to get there, and Klaus is even farther away."

****

From a distance, Liddy spotted the demolished bus that rested among a large swath of damaged buildings. Only a few people had come out from the widespread wreckage. They tended to loved ones or wandered dazed and disoriented in search of people and possessions. The bus leaned to one side with its right wheels collapsed. Nearby, the pulsing red light of an emergency vehicle flashed.

Liddy's heart sank. She prayed for Willy and the children … and anyone else who might have been on the bus.

She stood a safe distance from the wreck and strained to see any signs of Willy. Someone with a fire extinguisher tried to put out the smoldering flames near the engine while two other men frantically tried to open the door to the bus. Her eyes burned from the thick smoke, as screams and calls for help from inside the bus got louder.

The closer Liddy got, the harder her heart pounded. Out of the corner of her eye, she recognized a familiar man standing in the crowd nearby. *Herr Keppler!*

"*Herr* Keppler, I didn't expect to see you here!" She coughed and wiped a mixture of soot and tears from her face.

"I was working late at the station when we got the alarm. We're not that far away. Of course, we—"

"Willy's on that bus! Please, you've got to help me find him."

From the look on Keppler's face, Liddy was sure that he would respond in earnest to her plea. "Let's try to find him," he said.

"My hunch is that he would be at the back of the bus. That's where he always likes to sit."

"Let's hope so. It's the front of the bus where there's the most damage." He pointed over toward where the driver had sat. The roof was completely blown off.

Keppler climbed up through the back door, with Liddy following. "Willy! Willy!" she called in desperation. When she heard faint cries for help, she knelt to assist two children who were on the floor. "Someone will be here soon to help you," she told them and followed after Keppler.

Keppler probed farther forward with his flashlight. "There he is, *Fräulein*! He's under a seat—still dazed."

"Willy!" Liddy screamed. She rushed to his side, kneeled, and cupped her hands around his cheeks. A deep gash on his forehead covered his face with blood.

"Are you all right?" Liddy asked him.

He moaned, his eyes now opening fully. "Oh, Liddy. Thank God you're here. Where's Father?"

"He's on his way. Just relax. We're going to get you out of here."

"My—My leg is pinned under this seat frame," Willy moaned. "I think it must be broken."

"We've got to get this frame off him," Keppler said. "It's still attached on the far end but loose on this end. I think I can lift it." He gave it a try, but it barely budged. "We're leaning at such a bad angle, we've got gravity working against us. It's not going to be easy." Deep creases of worry ran across Keppler's brow.

Liddy held Willy's hand. "You're going to be all right," she kept repeating. "Let's get your mind off all this. I know—imagine something nice like playing the piano." The image of that was far more pleasant to her senses than the smell of the oily smoke.

"But what about his other hand?" Keppler asked Liddy, his voice filled with deep concern.

She reached carefully to examine Willy's other hand.

"I—I think it's okay," Willy mumbled. "I have no pain in either hand, but—but my leg hurts real bad."

"Well, at least my little piano player's hands are fine," Liddy said. She was determined to add a positive note to the horrible scene.

But a moan from Willy soon took away that positive feeling. She looked down to see his eyes first close, then open. He was struggling to stay conscious.

"You must be in a lot of pain," she said. "Be brave." She looked back up at Keppler. "We must hurry!"

"I'm going to try to move this again," Keppler responded. He positioned himself for maximum leverage. He put one hand on the floor and pushed up with the other. The seat frame began to lift, but Liddy spotted some sharp bolts that protruded from the underside of the frame.

"Be careful of those bolts," she warned as she started to pull Willy's body out. She huffed and tugged and … slowly he began to move.

"He's free!" Liddy said. "Oh, thank God!"

"Yes, thank you, God," Keppler repeated. "Now we need to get him out of here."

Surprised at Keppler's words, Liddy stared at the man, and their eyes locked as the corners of his mouth turned up in a slight smile. A moment of understanding passed between the two, once adversaries but now partners together in an effort to free Willy from the tight confines of the bus.

Without warning, the bus shifted, and Keppler struggled to keep his grip on the seat.

In desperation, Liddy reached to help him. "Watch out!" she yelled.

The bus shifted again, and the seat frame started to slide back into place, right where Keppler's hand rested on the floor. Liddy lunged, covering his hand with her own just as the frame slammed back in place … and on her hand.

Liddy screamed in agony as a jagged bolt penetrated the top of her hand. Blood squirted everywhere.

"*Fraulein!*" Keppler said. "I'll lift the seat once more, and pull your hand out!" With his shoulder, he leveraged the seat up again.

Liddy pulled her hand free and just stared as blood gushed out.

"Here, let me wrap it up tight with my handkerchief," Keppler said as he reached into his pocket. He hurried to wind the cloth around Liddy's wound.

"Wait, I see a monogram. Isn't that Marek's handkerchief?" she asked, but there was no answer.

Dizzy from the pain and sight of blood, Liddy's eyes began to glaze over. A moment later, a familiar voice from outside the bus aroused her pain-filled senses.

"Liddy, Willy? Are you in there?"

"Marek, is that you?" Liddy yelled.

Keppler flashed his light toward the voice, and Liddy's heart flooded with joy when she saw Marek climbing aboard.

"Marek, how did you …?" She looked at Keppler, who smiled discreetly.

"Liddy, what's happened to you?" Marek glanced at Liddy's injured hand.

"A hand injury, but I'm going to be all right. Oh, Marek. I can't believe it's you in person!" Each flash of the ambulance's sterile light from behind Marek seemed to linger, turning into a warm glow around his head.

"Willy probably has a broken ..." Liddy did not finish her sentence. A loud voice from behind Marek interrupted them.

"That's the fellow—there's the *Tauscher*."

Marek snapped his head around in response. "I've been released by *Herr* Keppler," he asserted. "No, you don't understand."

"That was a mistake," came the stern response, along with gruff hands each side of him, grabbing his arms. "Come with us, Jew boy."

"What's happening?" Liddy implored. "No, this can't be! You must do something, *Herr* Keppler!" She scowled at him, met only by a puzzled stare. Her head turned frantically back around toward the door of the bus, but Marek was gone.

Liddy rushed to the door and screamed out into the chaos, "Stop! You can't take him. Help me, *Herr* Keppler. No, no—somebody stop them. Please. Marek!"

The flashing light glowed again, this time through a flood of tears now welling in her eyes, and overflowing down Liddy's cheeks.

****

With damage to flesh, muscle, and bone, Liddy would never knead bread dough again, but she could still do plenty of other chores to help around the Mittendorf family's establishment. *Herr* Keppler, his hand spared from harm, continued his exquisite piano playing and often helped Willy. As Willy and Liddy convalesced, Klaus quit his night job at the prison to devote full time to the bakery, ably assisted by Renate, but now without Marek.

One day, Liddy presented her father the printed picture book that she had compiled of historical buildings around Germany. It was indeed a bittersweet moment as she knew the book would not have been possible without Marek's help.

"I have a surprise for you, Father," Liddy had said on that day. She showed him a picture of *Grossvater* Mittendorf's restaurant the day it had opened. "Marek found this in the files at the newspaper."

"That's really quite something," her father said, his eyes moist.

"They worked hard, but it didn't succeed. That won't be the story for this Mittendorf establishment." She turned the page, showing a picture of the Mittendorf Bakery. Her father beamed and hugged Liddy tight. "*Meine Liebschen*, we will make it work," he exclaimed.

For the next several months, any worries about the survival of the bakery were for naught, as throngs of customers, many new, frequented the establishment. Word had spread around town about something unusual at the Mittendorfs' bakery. With mounting hardships brought on by the war, many craved more than just the delightful aroma of freshly baked pastries to start off their days. Also wafting through the air early each morning were the glorious notes of "Ave Maria," among other fine pieces, played to perfection by young Willy Mittendorf, prized pupil of *Herr* Conrad Keppler.

195

Discussion Questions

1. Liddy's phone call from Munich to her father in Berlin reveals what deep-seated longing?
2. Shy Liddy's following Marek on her bike seems out of character. What does it demonstrate?
3. What character traits make Herr Keppler similar to popular stereotypes of a Nazi police officer? In what way was he decidedly different?
4. What sort of risk was Klaus taking when he agreed to deliver letters from prison for Dietrich Bonhoeffer?
5. Why do you think Marek expressed a certain level of support for Nazism in front of Liddy?
6. What do you think was the most important thing Liddy and Marek learned about each other on the picnic?
7. Father Kolbe's focus on love in the midst of the evil around them was a good send-off for his people. Do you have examples of when love helped you through a particularly rough time?
8. Herr Keppler comments that the Gospels don't agree on everything. Can you name some differences? In light of the different audiences and times they were written, what is more striking—their similarities or dissimilarities?
9. In his dealings with Willy, Keppler exhibits personality characteristics such as punctuality, nationalism, and

perfection. When are these qualities good versus when can they turn bad?

10. What Scripture passages are cited as suggested resources when our backs are against the wall with some difficult situation?

11. The premise of the story is that Keppler's heart is redeemable. Do you think there is a point where evil is so entrenched, it is beyond hope?

12. In Liddy's letter to her *Grossmutter*, she does not mention listening to the BBC with her father. Why might that be?

13. Liddy poses a question to Keppler about what would please him the most. He avoids answering, but which of the choices do you think he would choose? How would he prioritize God, country, and family?

14. Are you surprised Liddy and her parents didn't address the possibility that Marek was Jewish before it came to a critical head? Why or why not?

15. Has fully comprehending God's love for you freed you up from fear in your life? Do you think it makes it easier to love others?

16. Keppler was a strategic thinker. How did his attempt to trap Liddy backfire?

17. Why did Keppler have such a hard time forgiving God?

18. Why was it important to the story's resolution that Liddy's act of love happen before she knew Keppler had released Marek? Was Marek's recapture consistent with the times?

Postscript – Historical Background

Brief Summary of World War II

The Rise of Hitler

Adolf Hitler and the Third Reich rose to power in the early 1930s as Germany struggled to find its identity following World War I, which ended in 1918. Penalties after that war left Germany very weak, and many looked for a bold leader who could restore Germany to world prominence. Few foresaw the evil that Hitler would eventually perpetrate. Along with his military goals, he also desired to elevate the Aryan (white) race. He deemed others, such as Jews, blacks, homosexuals, the mentally ill, and the handicapped, as not only inferior but also expendable.

Early Years of Aggression (1939–1941)

In September 1939, Germany invaded Poland, which caused Britain and France, along with some other countries, to declare war on Germany. Hitler then continued his aggression when he annexed or invaded several other European countries, including France. He was joined as an Axis power by Italian dictator Mussolini. Meanwhile, Stalin, of the Soviet Union, was also aggressive as he annexed small countries to his west. The Soviets, however, joined the Allied powers, which included Britain, France, and later the United States.

In August 1941, the German air force began a series of bombing strikes against mainland Britain. Countries in northern Africa also became battlegrounds. The Germans pushed eastward, with campaigns against key Soviet cities; however, harsh winter conditions hampered their success. Hitler was not aware that the Japanese would attack Pearl Harbor, Hawaii in December 1941, an event that would cause the United States to declare war on Japan. The Japanese then joined the Axis powers. Hitler declared war on the United States, which to this point had resisted direct war involvement.

Mid-War Years (1942–1943)

The American General Dwight D. Eisenhower took command of the Allied forces in 1942, and 1943 was marked by heavy bombing of Hamburg, Berlin, and other German cities by both Britain and the United States. On the ground, the recapture of Italy became a major initiative. During that time, numerous battles were also waged in the Pacific against the Japanese.

The War Turns (1944–1945)

Mid-1944 was a turning point in the war. The Allies recaptured Rome, Italy and succeeded in their quest for control of the beachhead at Normandy, France, after the D-Day landing. In August, the Allies liberated Paris, while the Soviets freed countries west of the USSR. In the spring of 1945, American troops advanced into Germany. Hitler, along with many of his military leaders, committed suicide soon thereafter. In May, Berlin surrendered to the Soviets, who had advanced from the east. On the Pacific front, the United States dropped two atomic bombs on Japan in August, which prompted the Japanese surrender. Fighting in all locations ratcheted down, but it wasn't until December 1946 that President Harry Truman declared the end of all hostilities.

Post-War

After the war, the Allies divided Germany into East and West sections, with control given to the different victors. Berlin, located in East Germany, was divided into four sectors. The Berlin Wall, which would divide the city, was erected in 1961. A symbolic separation of democracy and communism, it was not taken down until 1989.

Author's Notes

The preceding fictional story, which takes place during World War II, makes references to, or alludes to, a number of actual figures who played important roles during that war: Dietrich Bonhoeffer, Otto Jodmin, Maximilian Kolbe, Helmuth James Graf von Moltke, Freya von Moltke, Paul Reckzeh, Johanna Solf, Betsie and Corrie ten Boom, and Elisabeth von Thadden. All of these people, except Paul Reckzeh, were active in confronting the evil of the times—several of the thousands who put their lives in peril doing so.

A few disclaimers by the author are in order. As with other fictional stories, certain artistic liberties were taken in the way the historical figures were characterized. Any representations not based on fact that are perceived as disparaging are totally unintended.

Also, although the course of events described in the story is, in general, consistent with actual historical timelines in terms of the order in which they occurred, they may not align in all respects. The primary intent was to demonstrate the overall significant contributions of the historical figures and not to deal with precise related details such as exact dates that one might otherwise find documented in a biography.

Finally, the use of an *M* logo on Father Kolbe's newspapers and the description of a rundown building under the care of Otto Jodmin, are not based in fact but were used for dramatic effect only.

Historical Figures

Dietrich Bonhoeffer (1906–1945) has become one of the most admired Christian martyrs of the modern era. His focus on a down-to-earth relationship with Christ, genuine service-focused discipleship, and boldness in the face of evil have endeared him to countless people, both within and outside the Christian community.

Dietrich Bonhoeffer was born into a well-to-do family in Breslau, Germany, in 1906. His father was a renowned psychiatrist and professor at the University of Berlin. Dietrich grew up surrounded by a loving family, one of eight children, very much enjoying music and church teachings. As a teenager, he realized he wanted to study theology and pursued his education all the way to the doctorate level, attaining that degree by age twenty-one.

His early adult life included stints as vicar and lecturer at various locations around the world, including Spain and New York, where he attended Union Theological Seminary. While in the United States, he grew to greatly appreciate what were then termed Negro spirituals, many of which he brought back to friends in Germany. Later, he would pastor two German-speaking congregations in London.

As Hitler rose to power in the mid-1930s, Bonhoeffer often expressed disapproval, especially when the Protestant (Lutheran) German Church accepted Hitler's remolding of the church to the *Führer's* liking. Bonhoeffer took a leading role in the Confessing Church, which stood in opposition. Eventually banned from speaking in public, he often led spiritual discussions at secret conclaves of dissidents. He also authored several morally instructive books that are well read yet today, including *The Cost of Discipleship, Life Together: The Classic Exploration of Faith in Community,* and *Ethics.*

In order to avoid getting drafted into the military, Bonhoeffer became a member of the German *Abwehr*, comparable to the CIA. He joined other dissidents, including his brother-in-law, Hans von Dohnányi, as plots were formulated in secret to kill Hitler. One called Operation Flash failed when a bomb did not explode on an airplane. Later, the von Stauffenberg (Valkyrie) plot of July 20, 1944, also failed, as a bomb that did explode left Hitler uninjured.

In April 1943, Bonhoeffer and others of his family were arrested and sent to Tegel prison in Berlin. It took many months for the government to formalize charges of subversion. In the meantime, three guards, sympathetic to his cause, cooperated to smuggle letters and goods in and out of prison. Bonhoeffer also became engaged to Maria von Wedemeyer, but he never had the opportunity to marry her. It wasn't until September 1944, after almost one and a half years of imprisonment, that enough evidence was secured to determine the course of his final days.

Beginning in October, Bonhoeffer was moved to another prison and two concentration camps, ending with his execution by hanging at the age of thirty-nine at Flossenbürg concentration camp on April 9, 1945. It was only two weeks before American troops would liberate that concentration camp.

Thoughts and quotations attributed to Dietrich Bonhoeffer in the fictional story come from his entire body of work. No effort was made to limit them to his letters from prison. Actual quotations used or paraphrased include:

"Judging others makes us blind, whereas love is illuminating. By judging others we blind ourselves to our own evil and to the grace which others are just as entitled to as we are." —*The Cost of Discipleship*

202 D. P. Cornelius

"In normal life we hardly realize how much more we receive than we give, and life cannot be rich without such gratitude. It is so easy to overestimate the importance of our own achievements compared with what we owe to the help of others." —*Letters and Papers from Prison*

"If you board the wrong train, it is no use running along the corridor in the other direction." —*The Cost of Discipleship*

"I discovered later, and I'm still discovering right up to this moment, that it is only by living completely in this world that one learns to have faith. By this—worldliness—I mean living unreservedly in life's duties, problems, successes and failures. In so doing we throw ourselves completely into the arms of God, taking seriously, not our own sufferings, but those of God in the world. That, I think, is faith." —*Letters and Papers from Prison*

"Wait with me, I beg you! Let me embrace you long and tenderly, let me kiss you and love you and stroke the sorrow from your brow." —*Love Letters from Cell 92*

"Silence in the face of evil is itself evil: God will not hold us guiltless. Not to speak is to speak. Not to act is to act." — from book cover of Eric Metaxas' *Bonhoeffer: Pastor, Martyr, Prophet, Spy*

The remarkable act of charity of Maximilian Kolbe (1894–1941) in giving his life in exchange for another's was widely reported after the war by Franciszek Gajowniczek, the man whose life he saved. Kolbe's death marked the end of a life of significant accomplishment by this Franciscan monk who was born to a poor weaver.

The founder of the "City of Mary" (Immaculata) monastery at Niepokalanów, Poland, he established an almost self-sufficient city comprising baking and printing operations, and later a radio station. He published a daily newspaper, *The Knight*, which had a circulation of more than 230,000, along with a monthly magazine read by millions of Catholics in several countries. His early life included attainment of doctorates in both philosophy and theology. He also spent a major period in the 1930s as a missionary to Japan.

Arrested initially by the Nazis in September 1939 shortly after their invasion of Poland to start World War II, he was allowed to return three months later to reopen the monastery. His publishing, however, was curtailed, and his health continued to deteriorate.

After Kolbe took in about 1,500 Jewish refugees, the Nazis clamped down on him again, leading to his imprisonment at Auschwitz and ultimate death, which was witnessed and corroborated by several fellow prisoners who survived.

In 1971, Maximilian Kolbe was beatified by Pope Paul VI, and in 1982 Pope John Paul II, after an exhaustive review process, canonized him as Saint Kolbe, "Saint of Charity"—indeed, a true Christian martyr.

The quotation of Maximilian (Raymond) Kolbe paraphrased in this fictional story is:

"No one in the world can change Truth. What we can do and should do is to seek truth and to serve it when we have found it. The real conflict is the inner conflict. Beyond armies of occupation and the hetacombs of extermination camps, there are two irreconcilable enemies in the depth of every soul: good and evil, sin and love. And what use are the victories on the battlefield if we ourselves are defeated in our innermost personal selves?" —*Knight of Mary Immaculate*

Other Christian Resistance Leaders

Johanna Solf established her Solf Circle in 1936. Comprised of many intellectuals in Berlin society at the time, it was not originally intended to be actively subversive to the Nazi regime; however, it did grow to play a role in assisting Jewish refugees.

One of their events, a birthday party hosted by Elisabeth von Thadden in September 1943, was attended by a Gestapo infiltrator who subsequently betrayed the group by reporting the attendance of a large number of high-ranking dignitaries. Dr. Paul Reckzeh, a man who claimed to be a Swiss doctor, had deceived the group with his feigned anti-Nazi allegiance.

A leader of another group of intellectuals against the war, Helmuth James Graf von Moltke, was an internationally renowned attorney-at-law. He actually played a role in warning Frau Solf. A friend of Moltke's had informed Otto Kiep, a diplomat, about a taped telephone conversation that exposed delicate information. During this time, Moltke and his wife operated what was later called the Kreisau Circle, named after their summer estate.

Elisabeth von Thadden, also a member of the Solf Circle, had been headmistress of a famous boarding school for women that had been shut down by the Nazis. That school, which bears her name, still functions today.

All of these resistance people, and about seventy others were arrested in January 1944 and were ordered to appear before the People's Court (*Volksgerichtshof*). They were charged with conspiring to commit high treason or were otherwise directly implicated in a July 20, 1944, attempt on Hitler's life. By the following year, January 1945, all except Frau Solf and her daughter had been executed, along with thousands of other perceived perpetrators of treason. The Solfs temporarily escaped to Bavaria but were eventually imprisoned at Ravensbrück concentration camp. They both survived the war, and Johanna moved to England, where she died in 1955.

Also interned at Ravensbrück, in 1944, were the two Dutch sisters, Cornelia "Corrie" and Betsie ten Boom. Their family had harbored hundreds of Jews behind a secret wall in their watch repair shop. Betsie died at the concentration camp; however, Corrie—through a clerical error—was released and lived to tell her story of Christian faith and forgiveness through many lectures as well as her acclaimed book, *The Hiding Place*. She died in California in 1983.

Otto Jodmin was a caretaker of an apartment building in the wealthy neighborhood of Charlottenburg. Otto allowed refugees to use the cellar of his building and registered Jews as Aryans so they could get false identity papers and ration cards. He survived the war and later recollected, "I simply had to do it … I did not even think about it, not at all. I just couldn't act in any other way."[1]

---

[1]   Source: Morehouse, Roger. *Berlin at War*. New York: Basic Books, 2010, page 297.

Bibliography

Benge, Janet and Geoff. *Dietrich Bonhoeffer*. Seattle: YWAM Publishing, 2012.

von Bismarck, Ruth-Alice and Ulrich Itz. *Love Letters from Cell 92: The Correspondence Between Dietrich Bonhoeffer and Maria Von Wedemeyer, 1943-45*. Nashville: Abingdon Press, 1995.

Bonhoeffer, Dietrich. Letters and Papers from Prison. New York: Simon & Schuster, 1953.

Boyd, Gregory A. and Edward K. *Letters from a Skeptic*. Colorado Springs: Cook Common Ministries, 1994.

Frankl, Viktor E. *Man's Search for Meaning*. New York: Simon & Schuster, 1959.

Frossard, Andre. *Forget Not Love*. San Francisco: Ignatius Press, 1991.

The Holy Bible, New King James Version. Nashville: Thomas Nelson Publishers, 1982.

Metaxas, Eric. *Bonhoeffer: Pastor, Martyr, Prophet, Spy*. Nashville: Thomas Nelson, 2010.

Morehouse, Roger. *Berlin at War.* New York: Basic Books, 2010.

Stokesbury, James L. *A Short History of World War II.* New York: William Morrow & Co., 1980.

Von Moltke, Freya. *Memories of Kreisau.* Lincoln: University of Nebraska Press, 2003.

CPSIA information can be obtained
at www.ICGtesting.com
Printed in the USA
LVOW08s2306030217
523220LV00001B/68/P